Certain random remarks overheard by certain hapless canaries, on entering recklessly into certain odd cat houses . . .

"I might as well tell the story straight and pray to God that I can convince you that America doesn't want what we have discovered."

"All right, pipe down. The first one of you who lets on to anybody outside how good jail is ain't never getting back in!"

"The time has come, baby. Marie Antoinette has finally invited us to have a look at Versailles."

"Konigswasser and his body have just parted company, with his body wandering out of control into the lagoon and his psyche going off to watch the lions eat."

CANARY IN A CAT HOUSE

An Original Gold Medal Collection

by Kurt Vonnegut, Jr.

Gold Medal Books

Fawcett Publications, Inc., Greenwich, Conn.

Member of American Book Publishers Council, Inc.

Cover design and illustrations
by Leo and Diane Dillon

Contents

Report on the Barnhouse Effect

Let me begin by saying that I don't know any more about where Professor Arthur Barnhouse is hiding than anyone else does. Save for one short, enigmatic message left in my mail box on Christmas Eve, I have not heard from him since his disappearance a year and a half ago.

What's more, readers of this article will be disappointed if they expect to learn how *they* can bring about the so-called "Barnhouse Effect." If I were able and willing to give away that secret, I would certainly be something more important than a psychology instructor.

I have been urged to write this report because I did research under the professor's direction and because I was the first to learn of his astonishing discovery. But while I was his student I was never entrusted with knowledge of how the mental forces could be released and directed. He was unwilling to trust anyone with that information.

I would like to point out that the term "Barnhouse Effect" is a creation of the popular press, and was never used by Professor Barnhouse. The name he chose for the phenomenon was *"dynamopsychism,"* or *force of the mind.*

I cannot believe that there is a civilized person yet to be convinced that such a force exists, what with its destructive effects on display in every national capital. I think humanity has always had an inkling that this sort of force does exist. It has been common knowledge that some people are luckier than others with inanimate objects like dice. What Professor Barnhouse did was to show that such "luck" was a measurable force, which in his case could be enormous.

By my calculations, the professor was about fifty-five times more powerful than a Nagasaki-type atomic bomb at the time he went into hiding. He was not bluffing when, on the eve of "Operation Brainstorm," he told General Honus Barker: "Sitting here at the dinner table, I'm pretty sure I can flatten anything on earth—from Joe Louis to the Great Wall of China."

There is an understandable tendency to look upon Professor Barnhouse as a supernatural visitation. The First Church of Barnhouse in Los Angeles has a congregation numbering in the thousands. He is godlike in neither appearance nor intellect. The man who disarms the world is single, shorter than the average American male, stout, and averse to exercise. His I.Q. is 143, which is good but certainly not sensational. He is quite mortal, about to celebrate his fortieth birthday, and in good health. If he is alone now, the isolation won't bother him too much. He was quiet and shy when I knew him, and seemed to find more companionship in books and music than in his associations at the college.

Neither he nor his powers fall outside the sphere of Nature. His dynamopsychic radiations are subject to many known physical laws that apply in the field of radio. Hardly a person has not now heard the snarl of "Barnhouse static" on his home receiver. Contrary to what one might expect, the radiations are affected by sunspots and variations in the ionosphere.

However, his radiations differ from ordinary broadcast waves in several important ways. Their total energy can be brought to bear on any single point the professor chooses, and that energy is undiminished by distance. As a weapon, then, dynamopsychism has an impressive advantage over bacteria and atomic bombs, beyond the fact that it costs nothing to use: it enables the professor to single out critical individuals and objects instead of slaughtering whole populations in the process of maintaining international equilibrium.

As General Honus Barker told the House Military Affairs Committee: "Until someone finds Barnhouse, there is no defense against the Barnhouse Effect." Efforts to "jam" or block the radiations have failed. Premier Slezak could have saved himself the fantastic expense of his "Barnhouseproof" shelter. Despite the shelter's twelve-foot-thick lead armor, the premier has been floored twice while in it.

There is talk of screening the population for men potentially as powerful dynamopsychically as the professor. Senator Warren Foust demanded funds for this purpose last month, with the passionate declaration: "He who rules the Barnhouse Effect rules the world!" Commissar Kropotnik said much the same thing, so another costly armaments race, with a new twist, has begun.

This race at least has its comical aspects. The world's best gamblers are being coddled by governments like so many nuclear physicists. There may be several hundred persons with dynamopsychic talent on earth, myself included, but, without knowledge of the professor's technique, they can never be anything but dice-table despots. With the secret, it would probably take them ten years to become dangerous weapons. It took the professor that long. He who rules the Barnhouse Effect is Barnhouse and will be for some time.

Popularly, the "Age of Barnhouse" is said to have begun a year and a half ago, on the day of Operation Brainstorm. That was when dynamopsychism became significant politically. Actually, the phenomenon was discovered in May, 1942, shortly after the professor turned down a direct commission in the Army and enlisted as an artillery private. Like X-rays and vulcanized rubber, dynamopsychism was discovered by accident.

FROM time to time Private Barnhouse was invited to take part in games of chance by his barrack mates. He knew nothing about the games, and usually begged off. But one evening, out of social grace, he agreed to shoot craps.

It was a terrible or wonderful thing that he played, depending upon whether or not you like the world as it now is.

"Shoot sevens, Pop," someone said.

So "Pop" shot sevens—ten in a row to bankrupt the barracks. He retired to his bunk and, as a mathematical exercise, calculated the odds against his feat on the back of a laundry slip. His chances of doing it, he found, were one in almost ten million! Bewildered, he borrowed a pair of dice from the man in the bunk next to his. He tried to roll sevens again, but got only the usual assortment of numbers. He lay back for a moment, then resumed his toying with the dice. He rolled ten more sevens in a row.

He might have dismissed the phenomenon with a low whistle. But the professor instead mulled over the circumstances surrounding his two lucky streaks. There was one single factor in common: on both occasions, *the same thought train had flashed through his mind just before he threw the dice.* It was that thought train which aligned the professor's brain cells into what has since become the most powerful weapon on earth.

THE soldier in the next bunk gave dynamopsychism its first token of respect. In an understatement certain to bring wry smiles to the faces of the world's dejected demagogues, the soldier said, "You're hotter'n a two-dollar pistol, Pop." Professor Barnhouse was all of that. The dice that did his bidding weighed but a few grams, so the forces involved were minute; but the unmistakable fact that there were such forces was earth-shaking.

Professional caution kept him from revealing his discovery immediately. He wanted more facts and a body of theory to go with them. Later, when the atomic bomb was dropped on Hiroshima, it was fear that made him hold his peace. At no time were his experiments, as Premier Slezak called them, "a bourgeois plot to shackle the true democracies of the world." The professor didn't know where they were leading.

In time, he came to recognize another startling feature of dynamopsychism: *its strength increased with use.* Within six months, he was able to govern dice thrown by men the length of a barracks distant. By the time of his discharge in 1945, he could knock bricks loose from chimneys three miles away.

Charges that Professor Barnhouse could have won the last war in a minute, but did not care to do so, are perfectly senseless. When the war ended, he had the range and power of a 37-millimeter cannon, perhaps—certainly no more. His dynamopsychic powers graduated from the small-arms class only after his discharge and return to Wyandotte College.

I enrolled in the Wyandotte Graduate School two years after the professor had rejoined the faculty. By chance, he was assigned as my thesis adviser. I was unhappy about the assignment, for the professor was, in the eyes of both colleagues and students, a somewhat ridiculous figure. He missed classes or had lapses of memory during lectures. When I arrived, in fact, his shortcomings had passed from the ridiculous to the intolerable.

"We're assigning you to Barnhouse as a sort of temporary thing," the dean of social studies told me. He looked apologetic and perplexed. "Brilliant man, Barnhouse, I guess. Difficult to know since his return, perhaps, but his work before the war brought a great deal of credit to our little school."

When I reported to the professor's laboratory for the first time, what I saw was more distressing than the gossip. Every surface in the room was covered with dust; books and apparatus had not been disturbed for months. The professor sat napping at his desk when I entered. The only signs of recent activity were three overflowing ash trays, a pair of scissors, and a morning paper with several items clipped from its front page.

As he raised his head to look at me, I saw that his eyes were clouded with fatigue. "Hi," he said, "just can't seem to get my sleeping done at night." He lighted a cigarette, his hands trembling slightly. "You the young man I'm supposed to help with a thesis?"

"Yes, sir," I said. In minutes he converted my misgivings to alarm.

"You an overseas veteran?" he asked.

"Yes, sir."

"Not much left over there, is there?" He frowned. "Enjoy the last war?"

"No, sir."

"Look like another war to you?"

"Kind of, sir."

"What can be done about it?"

I shrugged. "Looks pretty hopeless."

He peered at me intently. "Know anything about international law, the U.N., and all that?"

"Only what I pick up from the papers."

"Same here," he sighed. He showed me a fat scrapbook packed with newspaper clippings. "Never used to pay any attention to international politics. Now I study them the way I used to study rats in mazes. Everybody tells me the same thing—'Looks hopeless.'"

"Nothing short of a miracle—" I began.

"Believe in magic?" he asked sharply. The professor fished two dice from his vest pocket. "I will try to roll twos," he said. He rolled twos three times in a row. "One chance in about 47,000 of that happening. There's a miracle for you." He beamed for an instant, then brought the interview to an end, remarking that he had a class which had begun ten minutes ago.

He was not quick to take me into his confidence, and he said no more about his trick with the dice. I assumed they were loaded, and forgot about them. He set me the task of watching male rats cross electrified metal strips to get to food or female rats—an experiment that had been done to everyone's satisfaction in the 1930s. As though the pointlessness of my work were not bad enough, the professor annoyed me further with irrelevant questions. His favorites were: "Think we should have dropped the atomic bomb on Hiroshima?" and "Think every new piece of scientific information is a good thing for humanity?"

HOWEVER, I did not feel put upon for long. "Give those poor animals a holiday," he said one morning, after I had been with him only a month. "I wish you'd help me look into a more interesting problem—namely, my sanity."

I returned the rats to their cages.

"What you must do is simple," he said, speaking softly. "Watch the inkwell on my desk. If you see nothing happen to it, say so, and I'll go quietly—relieved, I might add—to the nearest sanitarium."

I nodded uncertainly.

He locked the laboratory door and drew the blinds, so

that we were in twilight for a moment. "I'm odd, I know," he said. "It's fear of myself that's made me odd."

"I've found you somewhat eccentric, perhaps, but certainly not—"

"If nothing happens to that inkwell, 'crazy as a bedbug' is the only description of me that will do," he interrupted, turning on the overhead lights. His eyes narrowed. "To give you an idea of how crazy, I'll tell you what's been running through my mind when I should have been sleeping. I think maybe I can save the world. I think maybe I can make every nation a *have* nation, and do away with war for good. I think maybe I can clear roads through jungles, irrigate deserts, build dams overnigh*

"Yes, sir."

"Watch the inkwell!"

Dutifully and fearfully I watched. A high-pitched humming seemed to come from the inkwell; then it began to vibrate alarmingly, and finally to bound about the top of the desk, making two noisy circuits. It stopped, hummed again, glowed red, then popped in splinters with a blue-green flash.

Perhaps my hair stood on end. The professor laughed gently. "Magnets?" I managed to say at last.

"Wish to Heaven it were magnets," he murmured. It was then that he told me of dynamopsychism. He knew only that there was such a force; he could not explain it. "It's me and me alone—and it's awful."

"I'd say it was amazing and wonderful!" I cried.

"If all I could do was make inkwells dance, I'd be tickled silly with the whole business." He shrugged disconsolately. "But I'm no toy, my boy. If you like, we can drive around the neighborhood, and I'll show you what I mean." He told me about pulverized boulders, shattered oaks and abandoned farm buildings demolished within a fifty-mile radius of the campus. "Did every bit of it sitting right here, just thinking—not even thinking hard."

He scratched his head nervously. "I have never dared to concentrate as hard as I can for fear of the damage I might do. I'm to the point where a mere whim is a blockbuster." There was a depressing pause. "Up until a few days ago, I've thought it best to keep my secret for fear of what use it might be put to," he continued. "Now I realize that I haven't any more right to it than a man has a right to own an atomic bomb."

He fumbled through a heap of papers. "This says about all that needs to be said, I think." He handed me a draft of a letter to the Secretary of State.

Dear Sir:

I have discovered a new force which costs nothing to use, and which is probably more important than atomic energy. I should like to see it used most effectively in the cause of peace, and am, therefore, requesting your advice as to how this might best be done.

Yours truly,
A. Barnhouse.

'I have no idea what will happen next," said the professor.

THERE followed three months of perpetual nightmare, wherein the nation's political and military great came at all hours to watch the professor's tricks with fascination.

We were quartered in an old mansion near Charlottesville, Virginia, to which we had been whisked five days after the letter was mailed. Surrounded by barbed wire and twenty guards, we were labeled "Project Wishing Well," and were classified as Top Secret.

For companionship we had General Honus Barker and the State Department's William K. Cuthrell. For the professor's talk of peace-through-plenty they had indulgent smiles and much discourse on practical measures and realistic thinking. So treated, the professor, who had at first been almost meek, progressed in a matter of weeks toward stubbornness.

He had agreed to reveal the thought train by means of which he aligned his mind into a dynamopsychic transmitter. But, under Cuthrell's and Barker's nagging to do so, he began to hedge. At first he declared that the information could be passed on simply by word of mouth. Later he said that it would have to be written up in a long report. Finally, at dinner one night, just after General Barker had read the secret orders for Operation Brainstorm, the professor announced, "The report may take as long as five years to write." He looked fiercely at the general. "Maybe twenty."

The dismay occasioned by this flat announcement was offset somewhat by the exciting anticipation of Operation

Brainstorm. The general was in a holiday mood. "The target ships are on their way to the Caroline Islands at this very moment," he declared ecstatically. "One hundred and twenty of them! At the same time, ten V-2s are being readied for firing in New Mexico, and fifty radio-controlled jet bombers are being equipped for a mock attack on the Aleutians. Just think of it!" Happily he reviewed his orders. "At exactly 1100 hours next Wednesday, I will give you the order to *concentrate;* and you, professor, will think as hard as you can about sinking the target ships, destroying the V-2s before they hit the ground, and knocking down the bombers before they reach the Aleutians! Think you can handle it?"

The professor turned gray and closed his eyes. "As I told you before, my friend, I don't know what I can do." He added bitterly, "As for this Operation Brainstorm, I was never consulted about it, and it strikes me as childish and insanely expensive."

General Barker bridled. "Sir," he said, "your field is psychology, and I wouldn't presume to give you advice in that field. Mine is national defense. I have had thirty years of experience and success, Professor, and I'll ask you not to criticize my judgment."

The professor appealed to Mr. Cuthrell. "Look," he pleaded, "isn't it war and military matters we're all trying to get rid of? Wouldn't it be a whole lot more significant and lots cheaper for me to try moving cloud masses into drought areas, and things like that? I admit I know next to nothing about international politics, but it seems reasonable to suppose that nobody would want to fight wars if there were enough of everything to go around. Mr. Cuthrell, I'd like to try running generators where there isn't any coal or water power, irrigating deserts, and so on. Why, you could figure out what each country needs to make the most of its resources, and I could give it to them without costing American taxpayers a penny."

"Eternal vigilance is the price of freedom," said the general heavily.

Mr. Cuthrell threw the general a look of mild distaste. "Unfortunately, the general is right in his own way," he said. "I wish to Heaven the world were ready for ideals like yours, but it simply isn't. We aren't surrounded by brothers, but by enemies. It isn't a lack of food or resources that has us on the brink of war—it's a struggle for power. Who's going to be in charge of the world, our kind of people or theirs?"

The professor nodded in reluctant agreement and arose from the table. "I beg your pardon, gentlemen. You are, after all, better qualified to judge what is best for the country. I'll do whatever you say." He turned to me. "Don't forget to wind the restricted clock and put the confidential cat out," he said gloomily, and ascended the stairs to his bedroom.

For reasons of national security, Operation Brainstorm was carried on without the knowledge of the American citizenry which was footing the bill. The observers, technicians and military men involved in the activity knew that a test was under way—a test of what, they had no idea. Only thirty-seven key men, myself included, knew what was afoot.

In Virginia, the day for Operation Brainstorm was unseasonably cool. Inside, a log fire crackled in the fireplace, and the flames were reflected in the polished metal cabinets that lined the living room. All that remained of the room's lovely old furniture was a Victorian love seat, set squarely in the center of the floor, facing three television receivers. One long bench had been brought in for the ten of us privileged to watch. The television screens showed, from left to right, the stretch of desert which was the rocket target, the guinea-pig fleet, and a section of the Aleutian sky through which the radio-controlled bomber formation would roar.

Ninety minutes before H hour the radios announced that the rockets were ready, that the observation ships had backed away to what was thought to be a safe distance, and that the bombers were on their way. The small Virginia audience lined up on the bench in order of rank, smoked a great deal, and said little. Professor Barnhouse was in his bedroom. General Barker bustled about the house like a woman preparing Thanksgiving dinner for twenty.

At ten minutes before H hour the general came in, shepherding the professor before him. The professor was comfortably attired in sneakers, gray flannels, a blue sweater and a white shirt open at the neck. The two of them sat side by side on the love seat. The general was rigid and perspiring; the professor was cheerful. He looked at each of the screens, lighted a cigarette and settled back, comfortable and cool.

"Bombers sighted!" cried the Aleutian observers.

"Rockets away!" barked the New Mexico radio operator.

All of us looked quickly at the big electric clock over the mantel, while the professor, a half-smile on his face, continued to watch the television sets. In hollow tones, the general counted away the seconds remaining. "Five . . . four . . . three . . . two . . . one . . . *Concentrate!*"

Professor Barnhouse closed his eyes, pursed his lips, and stroked his temples. He held the position for a minute. The television images were scrambled, and the radio signals were drowned in the din of Barnhouse static. The professor sighed, opened his eyes and smiled confidently.

"Did you give it everything you had?" asked the general dubiously.

"I was wide open," the professor replied.

The television images pulled themselves together, and mingled cries of amazement came over the radios tuned to the observers. The Aleutian sky was streaked with the smoke trails of bombers screaming down in flames. Simultaneously, there appeared high over the rocket target a cluster of white puffs, followed by faint thunder.

General Barker shook his head happily. "By George!" he crowed. "Well, sir, by George, by George, by George!"

"Look!" shouted the admiral seated next to me. "The fleet—it wasn't touched!"

"The guns seem to be drooping," said Mr. Cuthrell.

We left the bench and clustered about the television sets to examine the damage more closely. What Mr. Cuthrell had said was true. The ships' guns curved downward, their muzzles resting on the steel decks. We in Virginia were making such a hullabaloo that it was impossible to hear the radio reports. We were so engrossed, in fact, that we didn't miss the professor until two short snarls of Barnhouse static shocked us into sudden silence. The radios went dead.

We looked around apprehensively. The professor was gone. A harassed guard threw open the front door from the outside to yell that the professor had escaped. He brandished his pistol in the direction of the gates, which hung open, limp and twisted. In the distance, a speeding government station wagon topped a ridge and dropped from sight into the valley beyond. The air was filled with choking smoke, for every vehicle on the grounds was ablaze. Pursuit was impossible.

"What in God's name got into him?" bellowed the general.

Mr. Cuthrell, who had rushed out onto the front porch, now slouched back into the room, reading a penciled note as he came. He thrust the note into my hands. "The good man left this billet-doux under the door knocker. Perhaps our young friend here will be kind enough to read it to you gentlemen, while I take a restful walk through the woods."

"*Gentlemen,*" I read aloud, "*As the first superweapon with a conscience, I am removing myself from your national defense stockpile. Setting a new precedent in the behavior of ordnance, I have humane reasons for going off. A. Barnhouse.*"

SINCE that day, of course, the professor has been systematically destroying the world's armaments, until there is now little with which to equip an army other than rocks and sharp sticks. His activities haven't exactly resulted in peace, but have, rather, precipitated a bloodless and entertaining sort of war that might be called the "War of the Tattletales." Every nation is flooded with enemy agents whose sole mission is to locate military equipment, which is promptly wrecked when it is brought to the professor's attention in the press.

Just as every day brings news of more armaments pulverized by dynamopsychism, so has it brought rumors of the professor's whereabouts. During last week alone, three publications carried articles proving variously that he was hiding in an Inca ruin in the Andes, in the sewers of Paris, and in the unexplored lower chambers of Carlsbad Caverns. Knowing the man, I am inclined to regard such hiding places as unnecessarily romantic and uncomfortable. While there are numerous persons eager to kill him, there must be millions who would care for him and hide him. I like to think that he is in the home of such a person.

One thing is certain: at this writing, Professor Barnhouse is not dead. Barnhouse static jammed broadcasts not ten minutes ago. In the eighteen months since his disappearance, he has been reported dead some half-dozen times. Each report has stemmed from the death of an unidentified man resembling the professor, during a period free of the static. The first three reports were followed at once by renewed talk of rearmament and recourse to war. The saber rattlers have learned how imprudent premature celebrations of the professor's demise can be.

Many a stouthearted patriot has found himself prone in the tangled bunting and timbers of a smashed reviewing stand, seconds after having announced that the archtyranny of Barnhouse was at an end. But those who would make war if they could, in every country in the world, wait in sullen silence for what must come—the passing of Professor Barnhouse.

To ASK how much longer the professor will live is to ask how much longer we must wait for the blessings of another world war. He is of short-lived stock: his mother lived to be fifty-three, his father to be forty-nine; and the life-spans of his grandparents on both sides were of the same order. He might be expected to live, then, for perhaps fifteen years more, if he can remain hidden from his enemies. When one considers the number and vigor of these enemies, however, fifteen years seems an extraordinary length of time, which might better be revised to fifteen days, hours or minutes.

The professor knows that he cannot live much longer. I say this because of the message left in my mailbox on Christmas Eve. Unsigned, typewritten on a soiled scrap of paper, the note consisted of ten sentences. The first nine of these, each a bewildering tangle of psychological jargon and references to obscure texts, made no sense to me at first reading. The tenth, unlike the rest, was simply constructed and contained no large words—but its irrational content made it the most puzzling and bizarre sentence of all. I nearly threw the note away, thinking it a colleague's warped notion of a practical joke. For some reason, though, I added it to the clutter on top of my desk, which included, among other mementos, the professor's dice.

It took me several weeks to realize that the message really meant something, that the first nine sentences, when unsnarled, could be taken as instructions. The tenth still told me nothing. It was only last night that I discovered how it fitted in with the rest. The sentence appeared in my thoughts last night, while I was toying absently with the professor's dice.

I promised to have this report on its way to the publishers today. In view of what has happened, I am obliged to break that promise, or release the report incomplete. The delay will not be a long one, for one of the few blessings accorded a bachelor like myself is the ability to move quickly from one abode to another, or from one way of life to another. What property I want to take with me can be packed in a few hours. Fortunately, I am not without substantial private means, which may take as long as a week to realize in liquid and anonymous form. When this is done, I shall mail the report.

I have just returned from a visit to my doctor, who tells me my health is excellent. I am young, and, with any luck at all, I shall live to a ripe old age indeed, for my family on both sides is noted for longevity.

Briefly, I propose to vanish.

Sooner or later, Professor Barnhouse must die. But long before then I shall be ready. So, to the saber rattlers of today—and even, I hope, of tomorrow—I say: Be advised. Barnhouse will die. But not the Barnhouse Effect.

Last night, I tried once more to follow the oblique instructions on the scrap of paper. I took the professor's dice, and then, with the last, nightmarish sentence flitting through my mind, I rolled fifty consecutive sevens.

Good-by.

All the
King's Horses

COLONEL BRYAN KELLY, his huge figure blocking off the
light that filtered down the narrow corridor behind him,
leaned for a moment against the locked door in an agony
of anxiety and helpless rage. The small Oriental guard
sorted through a ring of keys, searching for the one that
would open the door. Colonel Kelly listened to the voices
inside the room.

"Sarge, they wouldn't dare do anything to Americans,
would they?" The voice was youthful, unsure. "I mean,
there'd be hell to pay if they hurt—"

"Shut up. Want to wake up Kelly's kids and have them
hear you running off at the mouth that way?" The voice
was gruff, tired.

"They'll turn us loose pretty quick, whaddya bet,
Sarge?" insisted the young voice.

"Oh, sure, kid they love Americans around here. That's
probably what they wanted to talk to Kelly about, and
they're packing the beer and ham sandwiches into box
lunches for us right now. All that's holding things up

is they don't know how many with mustard, how many without. How d'ya want yours?"

"I'd just like to—"

"Shut up."

"Okay, I'd just—"

"Shut up."

"I'd just like to know what's going on, is all." The young corporal coughed.

"Pipe down and pass that butt along," said a third voice irritably. "There's ten good puffs left in it. Don't hog the whole thing, kid." A few other voices muttered in agreement.

Colonel Kelly opened and closed his hands nervously, wondering how he could tell the fifteen human beings behind the door about the nightmarish interview with Pi Ying and the lunatic ordeal they were going to have to endure. Pi Ying said that their fight against death would be no different, philosophically. _from_ what all of them, except Kelly's wife and children, had known in battle. In a cold way, it was true—no different, philosophically. But Colonel Kelly was more shaken than he had ever been in battle.

Colonel Kelly and the fifteen on the other side of the door had crash-landed two days before on the Asiatic mainland, after they had been blown off course by a sudden storm and their radio had gone dead. Colonel Kelly had been on his way, with his family, to a post as military attaché in India. On board the Army transport plane with them had been a group of enlisted men, technical specialists needed in the Middle East. The plane had come to earth in territory held by a Communist guerrilla chief, Pi Ying.

All had survived the crash—Kelly, his wife Margaret, his ten-year-old twin sons, the pilot and copilot, and the ten enlisted men. A dozen of Pi Ying's ragged riflemen had been waiting for them when they climbed from the plane. Unable to communicate with their captors, the Americans had been marched for a day through rice fields and near-jungle to come at sunset to a decaying palace. There they had been locked in a subterranean room, with no idea of what their fates might be.

Now, Colonel Kelly was returning from an interview with Pi Ying, who had told him what was to become of the sixteen American prisoners. _Sixteen_—Kelly shook his head as the number repeated itself in his hectic thoughts.

The guard prodded him to one side with his pistol and thrust the key into the lock, and the door swung open. Kelly stood silently in the doorway.

A cigarette was being passed from hand to hand. It cast its glow for an instant on each expectant face in turn. Now it lighted the ruddy face of the talkative young corporal from Minneapolis, now cast rugged shadows over the eye sockets and heavy brows of the pilot from Salt Lake, now bloomed red at the thin lips of the sergeant.

Kelly looked from the men to what seemed in the twilight to be a small hillock by the door. There his wife Margaret sat, with the blond heads of her sleeping sons cradled in her lap. She smiled up at him, her face misty white. "Darling—you're all right?" Margaret asked quietly.

"Yes, I'm all right."

"Sarge," said the corporal, "ask him what Pi Ying said."

"Shut up." The sergeant paused. "What about it, sir— good news or bad?"

KELLY stroked his wife's shoulder gently, trying to make the right words come—words to carry courage he wasn't sure he had. "Bad news," he said at last. "Rotten news."

"Well, let's have it," said the transport pilot loudly. Kelly supposed he was trying to reassure himself with the boom of his own voice, with brusqueness. "The worst he can do is kill us. Is that it?" He stood and dug his hands into his pockets.

"He wouldn't dare!" said the young corporal in a threatening voice—as though he could bring the wrath of the United States Army to bear on Pi Ying with a snap of his fingers.

Colonel Kelly looked at the youngster with curiosity and dejection. "Let's face it. The little man upstairs has all the trumps." An expression borrowed from another game, he thought irrelevantly. "He's an outlaw. He hasn't got a thing to lose by getting the United States sore at him."

"If he's going to kill us, say so!" the pilot said explosively. "So he's got us cold! What's he going to do?"

"He considers us prisoners of war," said Kelly, trying

to keep his voice even. "He'd like to shoot us all." He
shrugged. "I haven't been trying to keep you in suspense,
I've been looking for the right words—and there aren't
any. Pi Ying wants more entertainment out of us than
shooting us would provide. He'd like to prove that he's
smarter than we are in the bargain."

"How?" asked Margaret. Her eyes were wide. The two
children were waking up.

"In a little while, Pi Ying and I are going to play chess
for your lives." He closed his fist over his wife's limp
hand. "And for my four lives. It's the only chance
Pi Ying will give us." He shrugged, and smiled wryly. "I
play a better-than-average game—a little better than
average."

"Is he nuts?" said the sergeant.

"You'll all see for yourselves," said Colonel Kelly
simply. "You'll see him when the game begins—Pi Ying
and his friend, Major Barzov." He raised his eyebrows. "The major claims to be sorry that, in his ca-
pacity as a military observer for the Russian army, he
is powerless to intervene in our behalf. He also says we
have his sympathy. I suspect he's a damn' liar on both
counts. Pi Ying is scared stiff of him."

"We get to watch the game?" whispered the corporal
tensely.

"The sixteen of us, soldier, are the chessmen I'll be
playing with."

The door swung open. . . .

"Can you see the whole board from down there, White
King?" called Pi Ying cheerfully from a balcony overlooking the ornate, azure-domed chamber. He was smiling
down at Colonel Bryan Kelly, his family, and his men.
"You must be the White King, you know. Otherwise, we
couldn't be sure that you'd be with us for the whole
game." The guerrilla chief's face was flushed. His smile
was one of mock solicitousness. "Delighted to see all of
you!"

To Pi Ying's right, indistinct in the shadows, stood
Major Barzov, the taciturn Russian military observer. He
acknowledged Kelly's stare with a slow nod. Kelly continued to stare fixedly. The arrogant, bristle-haired major
became restless, folding and unfolding his arms, repeat-
edly rocking back and forth in his black boots. "I wish

I could help you," he said at last. It wasn't an amenity but a contemptuous jest. "I am only an observer here." Barzov said it heavily. "I wish you luck, Colonel," he added, and turned his back.

Seated on Pi Ying's left was a delicate young Oriental woman. She gazed expressionlessly at the wall over the Americans' heads. She and Barzov had been present when Pi Ying had first told Colonel Kelly of the game he wanted to play. When Kelly had begged Pi Ying to leave his wife and children out of it, he had thought he saw a spark of pity in her eyes. As he looked up at the motionless, ornamental girl now, he knew he must have been mistaken.

"This room was a whim of my predecessors, who for generations held the people in slavery," said Pi Ying sententiously. "It served nicely as a throne room. But the floor is inlaid with squares, sixty-four of them—a chessboard, you see? The former tenants had those handsome, man-sized chessmen before you built so that they and their friends could sit up here and order servants to move them about." He twisted a ring on his finger. "Imaginative as that was, it remained for us to hit upon this new twist. Today, of course, we will use only the black chessmen, my pieces." He turned to the restive Major Barzov. "The Americans have furnished their own chessmen. Fascinating idea." His smile faded when he saw that Barzov wasn't smiling with him. Pi Ying seemed eager to please the Russian. Barzov, in turn, appeared to regard Pi Ying as hardly worth listening to.

THE twelve American soldiers stood against a wall under heavy guard. Instinctively, they bunched together and glared sullenly at their patronizing host. "Take it easy," said Colonel Kelly, "or we'll lose the one chance we've got." He looked quickly at his twin sons, Jerry and Paul, who gazed about the room, unruffled, interested, blinking sleepily at the side of their stunned mother. Kelly wondered why he felt so little as he watched his family in the face of death. The fear he had felt while they were waiting in their dark prison was gone. Now he recognized the eerie calm—an old wartime friend—that left only the cold machinery of his wits and senses alive. It was the narcotic of generalship. It was the essence of war.

"Now, my friends, your attention," said Pi Ying importantly. He stood. "The rules of the game are easy to remember. You are all to behave as Colonel Kelly tells you. Those of you who are so unfortunate as to be taken by one of my chessmen will be killed quickly, painlessly, promptly." Major Barzov looked at the ceiling as though he were inwardly criticizing everything Pi Ying said.

The corporal suddenly released a blistering stream of obscenities—half abuse, half self-pity. The sergeant clapped his hand over the youngster's mouth.

Pi Ying leaned over the balustrade and pointed a finger at the struggling soldier. "For those who run from the board or make an outcry, a special form of death can be arranged," he said sharply. "Colonel Kelly and I must have complete silence in which to concentrate. If the colonel is clever enough to win, then all of you who are still with us when I am checkmated will get safe transport out of my territory. If he loses—" Pi Ying shrugged. He settled back on a mound of cushions. "Now, you must all be good sports," he said briskly. "Americans are noted for that, I believe. As Colonel Kelly can tell you, a chess game can very rarely be won—any more than a battle can be won—without sacrifices. Isn't that so, Colonel?"

Colonel Kelly nodded mechanically. He was recalling what Pi Ying had said earlier—that the game he was about to play was no different, philosophically, from what he had known in war.

"How can you do this to children!" cried Margaret suddenly, twisting free of a guard and striding across the squares to stand directly below Pi Ying's balcony. "For the love of God—" she began.

Pi Ying interrupted angrily: "Is it for the love of God that Americans make bombs and jet planes and tanks?" He waved her away impatiently. "Drag her back." He covered his eyes. "Where was I? We were talking about sacrifices, weren't we? I was going to ask you who you had chosen to be your king's pawn," said Pi Ying. "If you haven't chosen one, Colonel, I'd like to recommend the noisy young man down there—the one the sergeant is holding. A delicate position, king's pawn."

The corporal began to kick and twist with new fury. The sergeant tightened his arms about him. "The kid'll calm down in a minute," he said under his breath. He turned his head toward Colonel Kelly. "Whatever the hell the king's pawn is, that's me. Where do I stand, sir?" The youngster relaxed and the sergeant freed him.

Kelly pointed to the fourth square in the second row of the huge chessboard. The sergeant strode to the square and hunched his broad shoulders. The corporal mumbled something incoherent, and took his place in the square next to the sergeant—a second dependable pawn. The rest still hung back.

"Colonel, you tell us where to go," said a lanky T-4 uncertainly. "What do we know about chess? You put us where you want us." His Adam's apple bobbed. "Save the soft spots for your wife and kids. They're the ones that count. You tell us what to do."

"There are no soft spots," said the pilot sardonically, "no soft spots for anybody. Pick a square, any square." He stepped onto the board. "What does this square make me?"

"You're a bishop, Lieutenant, the king's bishop," said Kelly.

He found himself thinking of the lieutenant in those terms—no longer human, but a piece capable of moving diagonally across the board; capable, when attacking with the queen, of terrible damage to the black men across the board.

"And me in church only twice in my life. Hey, Pi Ying," called the pilot insolently, "what's a bishop worth?"

Pi Ying was amused. "A knight and a pawn, my boy; a knight and a pawn."

Thank God for the lieutenant, thought Kelly. One of the American soldiers grinned. They had been sticking close together, backed against the wall. Now they began to talk among themselves—like a baseball team warming up. At Kelly's direction, seeming almost unconscious of the meaning of their actions, they moved out onto the board to fill out the ranks.

Pi Ying was speaking again. "All of your pieces are in place now, except your knights and your queen, Colonel. And you, of course, are the king. Come, come. The game must be over before suppertime."

Gently, shepherding them with his long arms, Kelly led his wife and Jerry and Paul to their proper squares. He detested himself for the calm, the detachment with which he did it. He saw the fear and reproach in Margaret's eyes. She couldn't understand that he had to be

this way—that in his coldness was their only hope for
survival. He looked away from Margaret.

Pi Ying clapped his hands for silence. "There, good;
now we can begin." He tugged at his ear reflectively. "I
think this is an excellent way of bringing together the
Eastern and Western minds, don't you, Colonel? Here
we indulge the American's love for gambling with our ap-
preciation of profound drama and philosophy." Major
Barzov whispered impatiently to him. "Oh, yes," said Pi
Ying, "two more rules: We are allowed ten minutes a
move, and—this goes without saying—no moves may be
taken back. Very well," he said, pressing the button on
a stop watch and setting it on the balustrade, "the honor
of the first move belongs to the white men." He grinned.
"An ancient tradition."

"Sergeant," said Colonel Kelly, his throat tight, "move
two squares forward." He looked down at his hands.
They were starting to tremble.

"I believe I'll be slightly unconventional," said Pi Ying,
half turning his head toward the young girl, as though
to make sure that she was sharing his enjoyment. "Move
my queen's pawn forward two squares," he instructed a
servant.

Colonel Kelly watched the servant slide the massive
carving forward—to a point threatening the sergeant. The
sergeant looked quizzically at Kelly. "Everything okay,
sir?" He smiled faintly.

"I hope so," said Kelly. "Here's your protection . . .
Soldier," he ordered the young corporal, "step forward
one square." There—it was all he could do. Now there
was no advantage in Pi Ying's taking the pawn he threatened—the sergeant. Tactically it would be a pointless
trade, pawn for pawn. No advantage so far as good
chess went.

"This is very bad form, I know," said Pi Ying blandly.
He paused. "Well, then again, I'm not so sure I'd be wise
to trade. With so brilliant an opponent, perhaps I'd better play flawless chess, and forget the many temptations."
Major Barzov murmured something to him. "But it
would get us into the spirit of the game right off, wouldn't
it?"

"What's he talking about, sir?" asked the sergeant apprehensively.

Before Kelly could order his thoughts, Pi Ying gave the order. "Take his king's pawn."

"Colonel! What'd you do?" cried the sergeant. Two guards pulled him from the board and out of the room. A studded door banged shut behind them.

"Kill me!" shouted Kelly, starting off his square after them. A half-dozen bayonets hemmed him in.

IMPASSIVELY, the servant slid Pi Ying's wooden pawn onto the square where the sergeant had stood. A shot reverberated on the other side of the thick door, and the guards reappeared. Pi Ying was no longer smiling. "Your move, Colonel. Come, come—four minutes have gone already."

Kelly's calm was shattered, and with it went the illusion of the game. The pieces in his power were human beings again. The precious, brutal stuff of command was gone from Colonel Kelly. He was no more fit to make decisions of life and death than the rawest recruit. Giddily, he realized that Pi Ying's object was not to win the game quickly, but to thin out the Americans in harrowing, pointless forays. Another two minutes crept by as he struggled to force himself to be rational. "I can't do it," he whispered at last. He slouched now.

"You wish me to have all of you shot right now?" asked Pi Ying. "I must say that I find you a rather pathetic colonel. Do all American officers give in so easily?"

"Pin his ears back, Colonel," said the pilot. "Let's go. Sharpen up. Let's go!"

"You're in no danger now," said Kelly to the corporal. "Take his pawn."

"How do I know you're not lying?" said the youngster bitterly. "Now I'm going to get it!"

"Get over there!" said the transport pilot sharply. "No!"

The sergeant's two executioners pinned the corporal's arms to his sides. They looked up expectantly at Pi Ying.

"Young man," said Pi Ying solicitously, "would you enjoy being tortured to death, or would you rather do as Colonel Kelly tells you?"

The corporal spun suddenly and sent both guards sprawling. He stepped onto the square occupied by the pawn that had taken the sergeant, kicked the piece over, and stood there with his feet apart.

Major Barzov guffawed. "He'll learn to be a pawn yet," he roared. "It's an Oriental skill Americans could do well to learn for the days ahead, eh?"

Pi Ying laughed with Barzov, and stroked the knee of the young girl, who had been sitting, expressionless, at his side. "Well, it's been perfectly even so far—a pawn for a pawn. Let's begin our offensives in earnest." He snapped his fingers for the attention of the servant. "King's pawn to king three," he commanded. "There! Now my queen and bishop are ready for an expedition into white man's territory." He pressed the button on the stop watch. "Your move, Colonel." . . .

IT was an old reflex that made Colonel Bryan Kelly look to his wife for compassion, courage. He looked away again—Margaret was a frightening, heartbreaking sight, and there was nothing he could do for her but win. Nothing. Her stare was vacant, almost idiotic. She had taken refuge in deaf, blind, unfeeling shock.

Kelly counted the figures still surviving on the board. An hour had passed since the game's beginning. Five pawns were still alive, among them the young corporal; one bishop, the nervy pilot; two rooks; two knights—ten-year-old frightened knights; Margaret, a rigid, staring queen; and himself, the king. The missing four? Butchered—butchered in senseless exchanges that had cost Pi Ying only blocks of wood. The other soldiers had fallen silent, sullen in their own separate worlds.

"I think it's time for you to concede," said Pi Ying. "It's just about over, I'm afraid. Do you concede, Colonel?" Major Barzov frowned wisely at the chessmen, shook his head slowly, and yawned.

Colonel Kelly tried to bring his mind and eyes back into focus. He had the sensation of burrowing, burrowing, burrowing his way through a mountain of hot sand, of having to keep going on and on, digging, squirming, suffocated, blinded. "Go to hell," he muttered. He concentrated on the pattern of the chessmen. As chess, the ghastly game had been absurd. Pi Ying had moved with no strategy other than to destroy white men. Kelly had moved to defend each of his chessmen at any cost, had risked none in offense. His powerful queen, knights and rooks stood unused in the relative safety of the two rear rows of squares. He clenched and unclenched his fists in frustration. His opponent's haphazard ranks were wide open. A checkmate of Pi Ying's king would be possible, if only the black knight weren't dominating the center of the board.

"Your move, Colonel. Two minutes," coaxed Pi Ying.

And then Kelly saw it—the price he would pay, that they all would pay, for the curse of conscience. Pi Ying had only to move his queen diagonally, three squares to the left, to put him in check. After that he needed to make one more move—inevitable, irresistible—and then checkmate, the end. And Pi Ying would move his queen. The game seemed to have lost its piquancy for him; he had the air of a man eager to busy himself elsewhere.

The guerrilla chief was standing now, leaning over the balustrade. Major Barzov stood behind him, fitting a cigarette into an ornate ivory holder. "It's a very distressing thing about chess," said Barzov, admiring the holder, turning it this way and that. "There isn't a grain of luck in the game, you know. There's no excuse for the loser." His tone was pedantic, with the superciliousness of a teacher imparting profound truths to students too immature to understand.

Pi Ying shrugged. "Winning this game gives me very little satisfaction. Colonel Kelly has been a disappointment. By risking nothing, he had deprived the game of its subtlety and wit. I could expect more brilliance from my cook."

THE hot red of anger blazed over Kelly's cheeks, inflamed his ears. The muscles of his belly knotted; his legs moved apart. Pi Ying must not move his queen. If Pi Ying moved his queen, Kelly would lose; if Pi Ying moved his knight from Kelly's line of attack, Kelly would win. Only one thing might induce Pi Ying to move his knight—a fresh, poignant opportunity for sadism.

"Concede, Colonel. My time is valuable," said Pi Ying.

"Is it all over?" asked the young corporal querulously.

"Keep your mouth shut and stay where you are," said Kelly. He stared through shrewd, narrowed eyes at Pi Ying's knight, standing in the midst of the living chessmen. The horse's carved neck arched. Its nostrils flared.

The pure geometry of the white chessmen's fate burst upon Kelly's consciousness. Its simplicity had the effect

of a refreshing, chilling wind. A sacrifice had to be offered
to Pi Ying's knight. If Pi Ying accepted the sacrifice, the
game would be Kelly's. The trap was perfect and deadly
save for one detail—bait.

"One minute, Colonel," said Pi Ying.

Kelly looked quickly from face to face, unmoved by
the hostility or distrust or fear that he saw in each pair of
eyes. One by one he eliminated the candidates for death.
These four were vital to the sudden, crushing offense, and
these must guard the king. Necessity, like a child counting eeny, meeny, miney, moe around a circle, pointed its
finger at the one chessman who could be sacrificed.
There was only one.

Kelly didn't permit himself to think of the chessman as
anything but a cipher in a rigid mathematical proposition:
if x is dead, the rest shall live. He perceived the tragedy
of his decision only as a man who knew the definition of
tragedy, not as one who felt it.

"Twenty seconds!" said Barzov. He had taken the stop
watch from Pi Ying.

The cold resolve deserted Kelly for an instant, and
he saw the utter pathos of his position—a dilemma as
old as mankind, as new as the struggle between East and
West. When human beings are attacked, x, multiplied by
hundreds or thousands, must die—sent to death by
those who love them most. Kelly's profession was the
choosing of x.

"Ten seconds," said Barzov.

"Jerry," said Kelly, his voice loud and sure, "move
forward one square and two to your left." Trustingly,
his son stepped out of the back rank and into the shadow of the black knight. Awareness seemed to be filtering
back into Margaret's eyes. She turned her head when
her husband spoke.

Pi Ying stared down at the board in bafflement. "Are
you in your right mind, Colonel?" he asked at last. "Do
you realize what you've just done?"

A faint smile crossed Barzov's face. He bent forward
as though to whisper to Pi Ying, but apparently thought
better of it. He leaned back against a pillar to watch
Kelly's every move through a gauze of cigarette smoke.

Kelly pretended to be mystified by Pi Ying's words.
And then he buried his face in his hands and gave an
agonized cry. "Oh, God, no!"

"An exquisite mistake, to be sure," said Pi Ying. He excitedly explained the blunder to the young girl beside him. She turned away. He seemed infuriated by the gesture.

"You've got to let me take him back," begged Kelly brokenly.

Pi Ying rapped on the balustrade with his knuckles. "Without rules, my friend, games become nonsense. We agreed that all moves would be final, and so they are." He motioned to a servant. "King's knight to king's bishop six!" The servant moved the piece onto the square where Jerry stood. The bait was taken, the game was Colonel Kelly's from here on in.

"What is he talking about?" murmured Margaret.

"Why keep your wife in suspense, Colonel?" said Pi Ying. "Be a good husband and answer her question, or should I?"

"Your husband sacrificed a knight," said Barzov, his voice overriding Pi Ying's. "You've just lost your son." His expression was that of an experimenter, keen, expectant, entranced.

Kelly heard the choking sound in Margaret's throat, caught her as she fell. He rubbed her wrists. "Darling, please—listen to me!" He shook her more roughly than he had intended. Her reaction was explosive. Words cascaded from her—hysterical babble condemning him. Kelly locked her wrists together in his hands and listened dumbly to her broken abuse.

Pi Ying's eyes bulged, transfixed by the fantastic drama below, oblivious of the tearful frenzy of the young girl behind him. She tugged at his blouse, pleading. He pushed her back without looking away from the board.

The tall T-4 suddenly dived at the nearest guard, driving his shoulder into the man's chest, his fist into his belly. Pi Ying's soldiers converged, hammered him to the floor and dragged him back to his square.

In the midst of the bedlam, Jerry burst into tears and raced terrified to his father and mother. Kelly freed Margaret, who dropped to her knees to hug the quaking child. Paul, Jerry's twin, held his ground, trembled, stared stolidly at the floor.

"Shall we get on with the game, Colonel?" asked Pi Ying, his voice high. Barzov turned his back to the board, unwilling to prevent the next step, apparently reluctant to watch it.

Kelly closed his eyes, and waited for Pi Ying to give the order to the executioners. He couldn't bring himself to look at Margaret and Jerry. Pi Ying waved his hand for silence. "It is with deep regret—" he began. His lips closed. The menace suddenly went out of his face, leaving only surprise and stupidity. The small man slumped on the balustrade, slithered over it to crash among his soldiers.

Major Barzov struggled with the Chinese girl. In her small hand, still free of his grasp, was a slender knife. She drove it into her breast and fell against the major. Barzov let her fall. He strode to the balustrade. "Keep the prisoners where they are!" he shouted at the guards. "Is he alive?" There was no anger in his voice, no sorrow —only irritation, resentment of inconvenience. A servant looked up and shook his head.

Barzov ordered servants and soldiers to carry out the bodies of Pi Ying and the girl. It was more the act of a scrupulous housekeeper than a pious mourner. No one questioned his brisk authority.

"So this is your party after all," said Kelly.

"The peoples of Asia have lost a very great leader," Barzov said severely. He smiled at Kelly oddly. "Though he wasn't without weaknesses, was he, Colonel?" He shrugged. "However, you've won only the initiative, not the game; and now you have me to reckon with instead of Pi Ying. Stay where you are, Colonel. I'll be back shortly."

He ground out his cigarette on the ornamented balustrade, returned the holder to his pocket with a flourish, and disappeared through the curtains.

"Is Jerry going to be all right?" whispered Margaret. It was a plea, not a question, as though mercy were Kelly's to dole out or to withhold.

"Only Barzov knows," he said. He was bursting to explain the moves to her, to make her understand why he had had no choice; but he knew that an explanation would only make the tragedy infinitely more cruel for her. Death through a blunder she might be able to understand; but death as a product of cool reason, a step in logic, she could never accept. Rather than accept it, she would have had them all die.

"Only Barzov knows," he repeated wearily. The bargain was still in force, the price of victory agreed to. Barzov apparently had yet to realize what it was that Kelly was buying with a life.

"How do we know Barzov will let us go if we do win?" said the T-4.

"We don't, soldier. We don't." And then another doubt began to worm into his consciousness. Perhaps he had won no more than a brief reprieve. . . .

Colonel Kelly had lost track of how long they'd waited there on the chessboard for Barzov's return. His nerves were deadened by surge after surge of remorse and by the steady pressure of terrible responsibility. His consciousness had lapsed into twilight. Margaret slept in utter exhaustion, with Jerry, his life yet to be claimed, in her arms. Paul had curled up on his square, covered by the young corporal's field jacket. On what had been Jerry's square, the horse's carved head snarling as though fire would burst from its nostrils, stood Pi Ying's black knight.

KELLY barely heard the voice from the balcony—mistook it for another jagged fragment in a nightmare. His mind attached no sense to the words, heard only their sound. And then he opened his eyes and saw Major Barzov's lips moving. He saw the arrogant challenge in his eyes, understood the words. "Since so much blood has been shed in this game, it would be a pitiful waste to leave it unresolved."

Barzov settled regally on Pi Ying's cushions, his black boots crossed. "I propose to beat you, Colonel, and I will be surprised if you give me trouble. It would be very upsetting to have you win by the transparent ruse that fooled Pi Ying. It isn't that easy any more. You're playing me now, Colonel. You won the initiative for a moment. I'll take it and the game now, without any more delay."

Kelly rose to his feet, his great frame monumental above the white chessmen sitting on the squares about him. Major Barzov wasn't above the kind of entertainment Pi Ying had found so diverting. But Kelly sensed the difference between the major's demeanor and that of the guerrilla chief. The major was resuming the game, not because he liked it, but because he wanted to prove that he was one hell of a bright fellow, and that the Americans were dirt. Apparently, he didn't realize that Pi Ying had already lost the game. Either that, or Kelly had miscalculated.

In his mind, Kelly moved every piece on the board, driving his imagination to show him the flaw in his plan, if a flaw existed—if the hellish, heartbreaking sacrifice was for nothing. In an ordinary game, with nothing at stake but bits of wood, he would have called upon his opponent to concede, and the game would have ended there. But now, playing for flesh and blood, an aching, ineradicable doubt overshadowed the cleancut logic of the outcome. Kelly dared not reveal that he planned to attack and win in three moves—not until he had made the moves, not until Barzov had lost every chance to exploit the flaw, if there was one.

"What about Jerry?" cried Margaret.

"Jerry? Oh, of course, the little boy. Well, what about Jerry, Colonel?" asked Barzov. "I'll make a special concession, if you like. Would you want to take the move back?" The major was urbane, a caricature of cheerful hospitality.

"Without rules, Major, games become nonsense," said Kelly flatly. "I'd be the last to ask you to break them."

Barzov's expression became one of profound sympathy. "Your husband, madame, has made the decision, not I." He pressed the button on the stop watch. "You may keep the boy with you until the Colonel has fumbled all of your lives away. Your move, Colonel. Ten minutes."

"Take his pawn," Kelly ordered Margaret. She didn't move. "Margaret! Do you hear me?"

"Help her, Colonel, help her," chided Barzov.

Kelly took Margaret by the elbow, led her unresisting to the square where a black pawn stood. Jerry tagged along, keeping his mother between himself and Kelly. Kelly returned to his square, dug his hands into his pockets, and watched a servant take the black pawn from the board. "Check, Major. Your king is in check."

Barzov raised an eyebrow. "Check, did you say? What shall I do about this annoyance? How shall I get you back to some of the more interesting problems on the board?" He gestured to a servant. "Move my king over one square to the left."

"Move diagonally one square toward me, Lieutenant,"

Kelly ordered the pilot. The pilot hesitated. "Move! Do you hear?"

"Yessir." The tone was mocking. "Retreating, eh, sir?" The lieutenant slouched into the square, slowly, insolently.

"Check again, Major," Kelly said evenly. He motioned at the lieutenant. "Now my bishop has your king in check." He closed his eyes and told himself again and again that he had made no miscalculation, that the sacrifice *had* won the game, that there *could* be no out for Barzov. This was it—the last of the three moves.

"Well," said Barzov, "is that the best you can do? I'll simply move my queen in front of my king." The servant moved the piece. "Now it will be a different story."

"Take his queen," said Kelly to his farthest-advanced pawn, the battered T-4.

Barzov jumped to his feet. "Wait!"

"You didn't see it? You'd like to take it back?" taunted Kelly.

BARZOV paced back and forth on his balcony, breathing hard. "Of course I saw it!"

"It was the only thing you could do to save your king," said Kelly. "You may take it back if you like, but you'll find it's the only move you can make."

"Take the queen and get on with the game," shouted Barzov. "Take her!"

"Take her," echoed Kelly, and the servant trundled the huge piece to the side lines. The T-4 now stood blinking at Barzov's king, inches away. Colonel Kelly said it very softly this time: "Check."

Barzov exhaled in exasperation. "Check indeed." His voice grew louder. "No credit to you, Colonel Kelly, but to the monumental stupidity of Pi Ying."

"And that's the game, Major."

The T-4 laughed idiotically, the corporal sat down, the lieutenant threw his arms around Colonel Kelly. The two children gave a cheer. Only Margaret stood fast, still rigid, frightened.

"The price of your victory, of course, has yet to be paid," said Barzov acidly. "I presume you're ready to pay now?"

Kelly whitened. "That was the understanding, if it would give you satisfaction to hold me to it."

Barzov placed another cigarette in his ivory holder, taking a scowling minute to do it. When he spoke, it was in the tone of the pedant once more, the wielder of profundities. "No, I won't take the boy. I feel as Pi Ying felt about you—that you, as Americans, are the enemy, whether an official state of war exists or not. I look upon you as prisoners of war.

"However, as long as there is no official state of war, I have no choice, as a representative of my government, but to see that all of you are conducted safely through the lines. This was my plan when I resumed the game where Pi Ying left off. Your being freed has nothing to do with my personal feelings, nor with the outcome of the game. My winning would have delighted me and taught you a valuable lesson. But it would have made no difference in your fates." He lighted his cigarette and continued to look at them with severity.

"That's very chivalrous of you, Major," said Kelly.

"A matter of practical politics, I assure you. It wouldn't do to precipitate an incident between our countries just now. For a Russian to be chivalrous with an American is a spiritual impossibility, a contradiction in terms. In a long and bitter history, we've learned and learned well to reserve our chivalry for Russians." His expression became one of complete contempt. "Perhaps you'd like to play another game, Colonel—plain chess with wooden chessmen, without Pi Ying's refinement. I don't like to have you leave here thinking you play a better game than I."

"That's nice of you, but not this evening."

"Well, then, some other time." Major Barzov motioned for the guards to open the door of the throne room. "Some other time," he said again. "There will be others like Pi Ying eager to play you with live men, and I hope I will again be privileged to be an observer." He smiled brightly. "When and where would you like it to be?"

"Unfortunately, the time and the place are up to you," said Colonel Kelly wearily. "If you insist on arranging another game, issue an invitation, Major, and I'll be there."

D. P.

EIGHTY-ONE small sparks of human life were kept in an orphanage set up by Catholic nuns in what had been the gamekeeper's house on a large estate overlooking the Rhine. This was in the German village of Karlswald, in the American Zone of Occupation. Had the children not been kept there, not been given the warmth and food and clothes that could be begged for them, they might have wandered off the edges of the earth, searching for parents who had long ago stopped searching for them.

Every mild afternoon the nuns marched the children, two by two, through the woods, into the village and back, for their ration of fresh air. The village carpenter, an old man who was given to thoughtful rests between strokes of his tools, always came out of his shop to watch the bobbing, chattering, cheerful, ragged parade, and to speculate, with idlers his shop attracted, as to the nationalities of the passing children's parents.

"See the little French girl," he said one afternoon. "Look at the flash of those eyes!"

"And look at that little Pole swing his arms. They love
to march, the Poles," said a young mechanic.

"Pole? Where do you see any Pole?" said the carpenter.

"There—the thin, sober-looking one in front," the other replied.

"Aaaaah. He's too tall for a Pole," said the carpenter.
"And what Pole has flaxen hair like that? He's a German."

The mechanic shrugged. "They're all German now, so
what difference does it make?" he said. "Who can prove
what their parents were? If you had fought in Poland,
you would know he was a very common type."

"Look—look who's coming now," said the carpenter,
grinning. "Full of arguments as you are, you won't argue
with me about *him*. There we have an American!" He
called out to the child. "Joe—when you going to win
the championship back?"

"Joe!" called the mechanic. "How is the Brown Bomber today?"

At the very end of the parade, a lone, blue-eyed colored boy, six years old, turned and smiled with sweet
uneasiness at those who called out to him every day. He
nodded politely, murmuring a greeting in German, the
only language he knew.

His name, chosen arbitrarily by the nuns, was Karl
Heinz. But the carpenter had given him a name that
stuck, the name of the only colored man who had ever
made an impression on the villagers' minds, the former
heavyweight champion of the world, Joe Louis.

"Joe!" called the carpenter. "Cheer up! Let's see those
white teeth sparkle, Joe."

Joe obliged shyly.

The carpenter clapped the mechanic on the back. "And
if *he* isn't a German too! Maybe it's the only way we can
get another heavyweight champion."

Joe turned a corner, shooed out of the carpenter's
sight by a nun bringing up the rear. She and Joe spent
a great deal of time together, since Joe, no matter where
he was placed in the parade, always drifted to the end.

"Joe," she said, "you are such a dreamer. Are all your
people such dreamers?"

"I'm sorry, sister," said Joe. "I was thinking."

"Dreaming."

"Sister, am I the son of an American soldier?"

"Who told you that?"

"Peter. Peter said my mother was a German, and my
father was an American soldier who went away. He said
she left me with you, and then went away too." There was
no sadness in his voice—only puzzlement.

Peter was the oldest boy in the orphanage, an embit-
tered old man of fourteen, a German boy who could remember his parents and brothers and sisters and home,
and the war, and all sorts of food that Joe found impossible to imagine. Peter seemed superhuman to Joe, like a
man who had been to heaven and hell and back many
times, and knew exactly why they were where they were,
how they had come there, and where they might have
been.

"You mustn't worry about it, Joe," said the nun.
"No one knows who your mother and father were. But
they must have been very good people, because you
are so good."

"What is an American?" said Joe.

"It's a person from another country."

"Near here?"

"There are some near here, but their homes are far,
far away—across a great deal of water."

"Like the river."

"More water than that, Joe. More water than you
have ever seen. You can't even see the other side. You
could get on a boat and go for days and days and still
not get to the other side. I'll show you a map sometime.
But don't pay any attention to Peter, Joe. He makes
things up. He doesn't really know anything about you.
Now, catch up."

JOE hurried, and overtook the end of the line, where he
marched purposefully and alertly for a few minutes. But
then he began to dawdle again, chasing ghostlike words
in his small mind: . . . soldier . . . German . . . American
. . . your people . . . champion . . . Brown Bomber . . .
more water than you've ever seen.

"Sister," said Joe, "are Americans like me? Are they
brown?"

"Some are, some aren't, Joe."

"Are there many people like me?"

"Yes. Many, many people."

"Why haven't I seen them?"

"None of them have come to the village. They have places of their own."

"I want to go there."

"Aren't you happy here, Joe?"

"Yes. But Peter says I don't belong here, that I'm not a German and never can be."

"Peter! Pay no attention to him."

"Why do people smile when they see me, and try to make me sing and talk, and then laugh when I do?"

"Joe, Joe! Look quickly," said the nun "See—up there, in the tree. See the little sparrow with the broken leg. Oh poor, brave little thing—he still gets around quite well. See him, Joe? Hop, hop, hippity hop."

ONE hot summer day, as the parade passed the carpenter's shop, the carpenter came out to call something new to Joe, something that thrilled and terrified him.

"Joe! Hey, Joe! Your father is in town. Have you seen him yet?"

"No, sir—no, I haven't," said Joe. "Where is he?"

"He's teasing," said the nun sharply.

"You see if I'm teasing, Joe," said the carpenter. "Just keep your eyes open when you go past the school. You have to look sharp, up the slope and into the woods. You'll see, Joe."

"I wonder where our little friend the sparrow is today," said the nun brightly. "Goodness, I hope his leg is getting better, don't you, Joe?"

"Yes, yes I do, sister."

She chattered on about the sparrow and the clouds and the flowers as they approached the school, and Joe gave up answering her.

The woods above the school seemed still and empty.

But then Joe saw a massive brown man, naked to the waist and wearing a pistol, step from the trees. The man drank from a canteen, wiped his lips with the back of his hand, grinned down on the world with handsome disdain, and disappeared again into the twilight of the woods.

"Sister!" gasped Joe. "My father—I just saw my father!"

"No, Joe—no you didn't."

"He's up there in the woods. I saw him. I want to go up there, sister."

"He isn't your father, Joe. He doesn't know you. He doesn't want to see you."

"He's one of my people, sister!"

"You can't go up there, Joe, and you can't stay here." She took him by the arm to make him move. "Joe—you're being a bad boy, Joe."

Joe obeyed numbly. He didn't speak again for the remainder of the walk, which brought them home by another route, far from the school. No one else had seen his wonderful father, or believed that Joe had.

Not until prayers that night did he burst into tears. At ten o'clock, the young nun found his cot empty.

UNDER a great spread net that was laced with rags, an artillery piece squatted in the woods, black and oily, its muzzle thrust at the night sky. Trucks and the rest of the battery were hidden higher on the slope.

Joe watched and listened tremblingly through a thin screen of shrubs as the soldiers, indistinct in the darkness, dug in around their gun. The words he overheard made no sense to him.

"Sergeant, why we gotta dig in, when we're movin' out in the mornin', and it's just maneuvers anyhow? Seems like we could kind of conserve our strength, and just scratch around a little to show where we'd of dug if there was any sense to it."

"For all you know, boy, there may *be* sense to it before mornin'," said the sergeant. "You got ten minutes to get to China and bring me back a pigtail. Hear?"

The sergeant stepped into a patch of moonlight, his hands on his hips, his big shoulders back, the image of an emperor. Joe saw that it was the same man he'd marveled at in the afternoon. The sergeant listened with satisfaction to the sounds of digging, and then, to Joe's alarm, strode toward Joe's hiding place.

Joe didn't move a muscle until the big boot struck his side. *"Ach!"*

"Who's that?" The sergeant snatched Joe from the ground, and set him on his feet hard. "My golly, boy, what you doin' here? Scoot! Go on home! This ain't no place for kids to be playin'." He shined a flashlight in Joe's face. "Doggone," he muttered. "Where you come from?" He held Joe at arm's length, and shook him gently, like a rag doll. "Boy, how you get here—swim?"

Joe stammered in German that he was looking for his father.

"Come on—how you get here? What you doin'? Where's your mammy?"

"What you got there, sergeant?" said a voice in the dark.

"Don't rightly know what to call it," said the sergeant. "Talks like a Kraut and dresses like a Kraut, but just look at it a minute."

Soon a dozen men stood in a circle around Joe, talking loudly, then softly, to him, as though they thought getting through to him were a question of tone.

EVERY time Joe tried to explain his mission, they laughed in amazement.

"How he learn German? Tell me that."

"Where your daddy, boy?"

"Where your mammy, boy?"

"Sprecken zee Dutch, boy? Looky there. See him nod. He talks it, all right."

"Oh, you're fluent, man, mighty fluent. Ask him some more."

"Go get the lieutenant," said the sergeant. "He can talk to this boy, and understand what he's tryin' to say. Look at him shake. Scared to death. Come here, boy; don't be afraid, now." He enclosed Joe in his great arms. "Just take it easy, now—everything's gonna be all-l-l-l right. See what I got? By golly, I don't believe the boy's ever seen chocolate before. Go on—taste it. Won't hurt you."

Joe, safe in a fort of bone and sinew, ringed by luminous eyes, bit into the chocolate bar. The pink lining of his mouth, and then his whole soul, was flooded with warm, rich pleasure, and he beamed.

"He smiled!"

"Look at him light up!"

"Doggone if he didn't stumble right into heaven! I mean!"

"Talk about displaced persons," said the sergeant, hugging Joe, "this here's the most displaced little old person I *ever* saw. Upside down and inside out and ever which way."

"Here, boy—here's some more chocolate."

"Don't give him no more," said the sergeant reproachfully. "You want to make him sick?"

"Naw, sarge, naw—don't wanna make him sick. No, sir."

"What's going on here?" The lieutenant, a small, elegant Negro, the beam of his flashlight dancing before him, approached the group.

"Got a little boy here, lieutenant," said the sergeant. "Just wandered into the battery. Must of crawled past the guards."

"Well, send him on home, sergeant."

"Yessir. I planned to." He cleared his throat. "But this ain't no ordinary little boy, lieutenant." He opened his arms so that the light fell on Joe's face.

The lieutenant laughed incredulously, and knelt before Joe. "How'd you get here?"

"All he talks is German, lieutenant," said the sergeant.

"Where's your home?" said the lieutenant in German.

"Over more water than you've ever seen," said Joe.

"Where do you come from?"

"God made me," said Joe.

"This boy is going to be a lawyer when he grows up," said the lieutenant in English. "Now, listen to me," he said to Joe, "what's your name, and where are your people?"

"Joe Louis," said Joe, "and you are my people. I ran away from the orphanage, because I belong with you."

The lieutenant stood, shaking his head, and translated what Joe had said.

The woods echoed with glee.

"Joe Louis! I *thought* he was awful big and powerful-lookin'!"

"Jus' keep away from that left—*tha's* all!"

"If he's Joe, he's sure found his people. He's got us there!"

"Shut up!" commanded the sergeant suddenly. "All of you just shut up. This ain't no joke! Ain't nothing funny in it! Boy's all alone in the world. Ain't no joke."

A small voice finally broke the solemn silence that followed. "Naw—ain't no joke at all."

"We better take the jeep and run him back into town, sergeant," said the lieutenant. "Corporal Jackson, you're in charge."

"You tell 'em Joe was a *good* boy," said Jackson.

"Now, Joe," said the lieutenant in German, softly, "you come with the sergeant and me. We'll take you home."

Joe dug his fingers into the sergeant's forearms. "Papa! No—papa! I want to stay with you."

"Look, sonny, I ain't your papa," said the sergeant helplessly. "I *ain't* your papa."

"Papa!"

"Man, he's glued to you, ain't he, sergeant?" said a soldier. "Looks like you ain't never goin' to pry him loose. You got yourself a boy there, sarge, and he's got hisself a papa."

The sergeant walked over to the jeep with Joe in his arms. "Come on, now," he said, "you leggo, little Joe, so's I can drive. I can't drive with you hangin' on, Joe. You sit in the lieutenant's lap right next to me."

THE group formed again around the jeep, gravely now, watching the sergeant try to coax Joe into letting go.

"I don't want to get tough, Joe. Come on—take it easy, Joe. Let go, now, Joe, so's I can drive. See, I can't steer or nothin' with you hanging on right there."

"Papa!"

"Come on, over to my lap, Joe," said the lieutenant in German.

"Papa!"

"Joe, Joe, looky," said a soldier. "Chocolate! Want some more chocolate, Joe? See? Whole bar, Joe, all yours. Jus' leggo the sergeant and move over into the lieutenant's lap."

Joe tightened his grip on the sergeant.

"Don't put the chocolate back in your pocket, man! Give it to Joe anyways," said a soldier angrily. "Somebody go get a case of D bars off the truck, and throw 'em in the back for Joe. Give that boy chocolate enough for the nex' twenny years."

"Look, Joe," said another soldier, "ever see a wrist watch? Look at the wrist watch, Joe. See it glow, boy? Move over in the lieutenant's lap, and I'll let you listen to it tick. Tick, tick, tick, Joe. Come on, want to listen?"

Joe didn't move.

The soldier handed the watch to him. "Here, Joe, you take it anyway. It's yours." He walked away quickly.

"Man," somebody called after him, "you crazy? You

paid fifty dollars for that watch. What business a little boy got with any fifty-dollar watch?"

"No—I ain't crazy. Are you?"

"Naw, I ain't crazy. Neither one of us crazy, I guess. Joe—want a knife? You got to promise to be careful with it, now. Always cut *away* from yourself. Hear? Lieutenant, when you get him back, you tell him always cut *away* from hisself."

"I don't want to go back. I want to stay with *papa*," said Joe tearfully.

"Soldiers can't take little boys with them, Joe," said the lieutenant in German. "And we're leaving early in the morning."

"Will you come back for me?" said Joe.

"We'll come back if we can, Joe. Soldiers never know where they'll be from one day to the next. We'll come back for a visit, if we can."

"Can we give old Joe this case of D bars, lieutenant?" said a soldier carrying a cardboard carton of chocolate bars.

"DON'T ask me," said the lieutenant. "I don't know anything about it. I never saw anything of any case of D bars, never heard anything about it."

"Yessir." The soldier laid his burden down on the jeep's back seat.

"He ain't gonna let go," said the sergeant miserably. "You drive, lieutenant, and me and Joe'll sit over there."

The lieutenant and the sergeant changed places, and the jeep began to move.

" 'By, Joe!"

"You be a good boy, Joe!"

"Don't you eat all that chocolate at once, you hear?"

"Don't cry, Joe. Give us a smile."

"Wider, boy—that's the stuff!"

"Joe, Joe, wake up, Joe." The voice was that of Peter, the oldest boy in the orphanage, and it echoed damply from the stone walls.

Joe sat up, startled. All around his cot were the other orphans, jostling one another for a glimpse of Joe and the treasures by his pillow.

"Where did you get the hat, Joe—and the watch, and

knife?" said Peter. "And what's in the box under your bed?"

Joe felt his head, and found a soldier's wool knit cap there. "Papa," he mumbled sleepily.

"Papa!" mocked Peter, laughing.

"Yes," said Joe. "Last night I went to see my papa, Peter."

"Could he speak German, Joe?" said a little girl wonderingly.

"No, but his friend could," said Joe.

"He didn't see his father," said Peter. "Your father is far, far away, and will never come back. He probably doesn't even know you're alive."

"What did he look like?" said the girl.

Joe glanced thoughtfully around the room. "Papa is as high as this ceiling," he said at last. "He is wider than that door." Triumphantly, he took a bar of chocolate from under his pillow. "And as brown as that!" He held out the bar to the others. "Go on, have some. There is plenty more."

"He doesn't look anything like that," said Peter. "You aren't telling the truth, Joe."

"My papa has a pistol as big as this bed, almost, Peter," said Joe happily, "and a cannon as big as this house. And there were hundreds and hundreds like him."

"Somebody played a joke on you, Joe," said Peter. "He wasn't your father. How do you know he wasn't fooling you?"

"Because he cried when he left me," said Joe simply. "And he promised to take me back home across the water as fast as he could." He smiled airily. "Not like the river, Peter—across more water than you've *ever* seen. He promised, and then I let him go."

The Manned
Missiles

I, MIKHAIL IVANKOV, stone mason in the village of Ilba in the Ukrainian Soviet Socialist Republic, greet you and pity you, Charles Ashland, petroleum merchant in Titusville, Florida, in the United States of America. I grasp your hand.

The first true space man was my son, Major Stepan Ivankov. The second was your son, Captain Bryant Ashland. They will be forgotten only when men no longer look up at the sky. They are like the moon and the planets and the sun and the stars.

I do not speak English. I speak these words in Russian, from my heart, and my surviving son, Alexei, writes them down in English. He studies English in school and German also. He likes English best. He admires your Jack London and your O. Henry and your Mark Twain. Alexei is seventeen. He is going to be a scientist like his brother Stepan.

He wants me to tell you that he is going to work on science for peace, not war. He wants me to tell you also

49

that he does not hate the memory of your son. He understands that your son was ordered to do what he did. He is talking very much, and would like to compose this letter himself. He thinks that a man forty-nine is a very old man, and he does not think that a very old man who can do nothing but put one stone on top of another can say the right things about young men who die in space.

If he wishes, he can write a letter of his own about the deaths of Stepan and your son. This is my letter, and I will get Aksinia, Stepan's widow, to read it to me to make sure Alexei has made it say exactly what I wish it to say. Aksinia, too, understands English very well. She is a physician for children. She is beautiful. She works very hard so she can forget sometimes her grief for Stepan.

I WILL tell you a joke, Mr. Ashland. When the second baby moon of the U.S.S.R. went up with a dog in it, we whispered that it was not really a dog inside, but Prokhor Ivanoff, a dairy manager who had been arrested for theft two days before. It was only a joke, but it made me think what a terrible punishment it would be to send a human being up there. I could not stop thinking about that. I dreamed about it at night, and I dreamed that it was myself who was being punished.

I would have asked my elder son Stepan about life in space, but he was far away in Guryev, on the Caspian Sea. So I asked my younger son. Alexei laughed at my fears of space. He said that a man could be made very comfortable up there. He said that many young men would be going up there soon. First they would ride in baby moons. Then they would go to the moon itself. Then they would go to other planets. He laughed at me, because only an old man would worry about such simple trips.

Alexei told me that the only inconvenience would be the lack of gravity. That seemed like a great lack to me. Alexei said one would have to drink out of nursing bottles, and one would have to get used to the feeling of falling constantly, and one would have to learn to control one's movements because gravity would no longer offer resistance to them. That was all. Alexei did not think such things would be bothersome. He expected to go to Mars soon.

Olga, my wife, laughed at me, too, because I was too

old to understand the great new Age of Space. "Two Russian moons shine overhead," she said, "and my husband is the only man on earth who does not yet believe it!"

But I went on dreaming bad dreams about space, and now I had information to make my bad dreams truly scientific. I dreamed of nursing bottles and falling, falling, falling and the strange movements of my limbs. Perhaps the dreams were supernatural. Perhaps something was trying to warn me that Stepan would soon be suffering in space as I had suffered in dreams. Perhaps something was trying to warn me that Stepan would be murdered in space.

Alexei is very embarrassed that I should say that in a letter to the United States of America. He says that you will think that I am a superstitious peasant. So be it. I think that scientific persons of the future will scoff at scientific persons of the present. They will scoff because scientific persons of the present thought so many important things were superstitions. The things I dreamed about space all came true for my son. Stepan suffered very much up there. After the fourth day in space, Stepan sometimes cried like a baby. I had cried like a baby in my dreams.

I am not a coward, and I do not love comfort more than the improvement of human life. I am not a coward for my sons, either. I knew great suffering in the war, and I understand that there must be great suffering before great joy. But when I thought of the suffering that must surely come to a man in space, I could not see the joy to be earned by it. This was long before Stepan went up in his baby moon.

I went to the library and read about the moon and the planets, to see if they were truly desirable places to go. I did not ask Alexei about them, because I knew he would tell me what fine times we would have on such places. I found out for myself in the library that the moon and the planets were not fit places for men or for any life. They were much too hot or much too cold or much too poisonous.

I said nothing at home about my discoveries at the library, because I did not wish to be laughed at again. I waited quietly for Stepan to visit us. He would not laugh at my questions. He would answer them scientifically. He had worked on rockets for years. He would know everything that was known about space.

STEPAN at last came to visit us, and brought his beautiful wife. He was a small man, but strong and broad and wise. He was very tired. His eyes were sunken. He knew already that he was to be shot into space. First had come the baby moon with the radio. Next had come the baby moon with the dog. Next would come the baby moons with the monkeys and the apes. After them would come the baby moon with Stepan. Stepan had been working night and day, designing his home in space. He could not tell me. He could not even tell his wife.

Mr. Ashland, you would have liked my son. Everybody liked Stepan. He was a man of peace. He was not a major because he was a great warrior. He was a major because he understood rockets so well. He was a thoughtful man. He often said that he wished that he could be a stone mason like me. He said a stone mason would have time and peace in which to think things out. I did not tell him that a stone mason thinks of little but stones and mortar.

I asked him my questions about space, and he did not laugh. Stepan was very serious when he answered me. He had reason to be serious. He was telling me why he was himself willing to suffer in space.

He told me I was right. A man would suffer greatly in space, and the moon and the planets were bad places for men. There might be good places, but they were too far for men to reach in a lifetime.

"Then, what is this great new Age of Space, Stepan?" I asked him.

"It will be an age of baby moons for a long time," he said. "We will reach the moon itself soon, but it would be very difficult to stay there more than a few hours."

"Then why go into space, if there is so little good out there?" I asked him.

"THERE is so much to be learned and seen out there," he said. "A man could look at other worlds without a curtain of air between himself and them. A man could look at his own world, study the flow of weather over it, measure its true dimensions." This last surprised me. I thought the dimensions of our world were well known. "A man out there could learn much about the wonderful showers of matter and energy in space," said Stepan. And he spoke of many other poetic and scientific joys out there.

I was satisfied. Stepan had made me feel his own great joy at the thought of all the beauty and truth in space. I understood at last, Mr. Ashland, why the suffering would be worth while. When I dreamed of space again, I would dream of looking down at our own lovely green ball, dream of looking up at other worlds and seeing them more clearly than they had ever been seen.

It was not for the Soviet Union but for the beauty and truth in space, Mr. Ashland, that Stepan worked and died. He did not like to speak of the warlike uses of space. It was Alexei who liked to speak of such things, of the glory of spying on earth from baby moons, of guiding missiles to their targets from baby moons, of mastering the earth with weapons fired from the moon itself. Alexei expected Stepan to share his excitement about thoughts of such childish violence.

Stepan smiled, but only because he loved Alexei. He did not smile about war, or the things a man in a baby moon or on the moon itself could do to an enemy. "It is a use of science that we may be forced to make, Alexei," he said. "But if such a war happens, nothing will matter any more. Our world will become less fit for life than any other in the solar system."

Alexei has not spoken well of war since.

Stepan and his wife left late that night. He promised to come back before another year had passed, but I never saw him alive again.

When news came that the Soviet Union had fired a man-carrying baby moon into space, I did not know that the man was Stepan. I did not dare to suspect it. I could not wait to see Stepan again, to ask him what the man had said before he took off, how he was dressed, what his comforts were. We were told that we would be able to hear the man speak from space at eight o'clock that night on the radio.

We listened. We heard the man speak. The man was Stepan.

Stepan sounded strong. He sounded happy. He sounded proud and decent and wise. We laughed until we cried, Mr. Ashland. We danced. Our Stepan was the most important man alive. He had risen above everyone, and now he was looking down, telling us what our world looked like; looking up, telling us what the other worlds looked like.

Stepan made pleasant jokes about his little house in the sky. He said it was a cylinder ten meters long and four meters in diameter. It could be very cozy. And Stepan told us that there were little windows in his house, and a television camera, and a telescope, and radar, and all manner of instruments. How delightful to live in a time when such things could be! How delightful to be the father of the man who was the eyes, ears, and heart in space for all mankind!

HE would remain up there for a month, he said. We began to count the days. Every night we listened to a broadcast of recordings of things Stepan had said. We heard nothing about his nosebleeds and his nausea and his crying. We heard only the calm, brave things he had said. And then, on the tenth night, there were no more recordings of Stepan. There was only music at eight o'clock. There was no news of Stepan at all, and we knew he was dead.

Only now, a year later, have we learned how Stepan died and where his body is. When I became accustomed to the horror of it, Mr. Ashland, I said, "So be it. May Major Stepan Ivankov and Captain Bryant Ashland serve to reproach us, whenever we look at the sky, for making a world in which there is no trust. May the two men be the beginning of trust between peoples. May they mark the end of the time when science sent our good, brave young men hurtling to meet in death."

I enclose a photograph of my family, taken during Stepan's last visit to us. It is an excellent picture of Stepan. The body of water in the background is the Black Sea.

Mikhail Ivankov

DEAR Mr. Ivankov:

Thank you for the letter about our sons. I never did get it in the mail. It was in all the papers after your Mr. Koshevoi read it out loud in the United Nations. I never did get a copy just for me. I guess Mr. Koshevoi forgot to drop it in the mailbox. That's all right. I guess that's the modern way to deliver important letters, just hand them to reporters. They say your letter to me is just about the most important thing that's happened lately, outside of the fact we didn't go to war over what happened between our two boys.

I don't speak Russian, and I don't have anybody right close by who does, so you'll have to excuse the English. Alexei can read it to you. You tell him he writes English very well—better than I do.

Oh, I could have had a lot of expert help with this letter, if I'd wanted it—people happy to write to you in perfect Russian or perfect English or perfect anything at all. Seems like everybody in this country is like your boy Alexei. They all know better than I do what I should say to you. They say I have a chance to make history, if I answer you back the right things. One big magazine in New York offered me two thousand dollars for my letter back to you, and then it turned out I wasn't even supposed to write a letter for all that money. The magazine people had already written it, and all I had to do was sign it. Don't worry. I didn't.

I tell you, Mr. Ivankov, I have had a bellyful of experts. If you ask me, our boys were experted to death. Your experts would do something, then our experts would answer back with some fancy billion-dollar stunt, and then your experts would answer that back with something fancier, and what happened finally happened. It was just like a bunch of kids with billions of dollars or billions of rubles or whatever.

You are lucky you have a son left, Mr. Ivankov. Hazel and I don't. Bryant was the only son Hazel and I had. We didn't call him Bryant after he was christened. We called him Bud. We have one daughter, named Charlene. She works for the telephone company in Jacksonville. She called up when she saw your letter in the paper, and she is the only expert about what I ought to say I've listened to. She's a real expert, I figure, because she is Bud's twin. Bud never married, so Charlene is as close as you can get to Bud. She said you did a good job, showing how your Stepan was a good-hearted man, trying to do what was right, just like anybody else. She said I should show you the same about Bud. And then she started to cry, and she said for me to tell you about Bud and the goldfish. I said, "What's the sense of writing somebody in Russia a story like that?" The story doesn't prove anything. It's just one of those silly stories a family will keep telling whenever they get together. Charlene said that was why I should tell it to you, because it would be cute and silly in Russia, too, and you would laugh and like us better.

So here goes. When Bud and Charlene were about eight, why I came home one night with a fish bowl and two goldfish. There was one goldfish for each twin, only it was impossible to tell one fish from the other one. They were exactly alike. So one morning Bud got up early, and there was one goldfish floating on top of the water dead. So Bud went and woke up Charlene, and he said, "Hey, Charlene—your goldfish just died." That's the story Charlene asked me to tell you, Mr. Ivankov.

I THINK it is interesting that you are a mason. That is a good trade. You talk as if you lay up mostly stone. There aren't many people left in America who can really lay up stone. It's almost all cement-block work and bricks here. It probably is over there, too. I don't mean to say Russia isn't modern. I know it is.

Bud and I laid up quite a bit of block when we built the gas station here, with an apartment up over it. If you looked at the first course of block along the back wall, you would have to laugh, because you can see how Bud and I learned as we went. It's strong enough, but it sure looks lousy. One thing wasn't so funny. When we were hanging the rails for the overhead door, Bud slipped on the ladder, and he grabbed a sharp edge on the mounting bracket, and he cut a tendon on his hand. He was scared to death his hand would be crippled, and that would keep him out of the Air Force. His hand had to be operated on three times before it was right again, and every operation hurt something awful. But Bud would have let them operate a hundred times, if they had to, because there was just one thing he wanted to be, and that was a flyer.

One reason I wish your Mr. Koshevoi had thought to mail me your letter was the picture you sent with it. The newspapers got that, too, and it didn't come out too clear in the papers. But one thing we couldn't get over was all that beautiful water behind you. Somehow, when we think about Russia, we never think about any water

round. I guess that shows how ignorant we are. Hazel
and I live up over the gas station, and we can see water,
too. We can see the Atlantic Ocean, or an inlet of it
they call Indian River. We can see Merritt Island, too,
out in the water, and we can see the place Bud's rocket
went up from. It is called Cape Canaveral. I guess you
know that. It isn't any secret where he went up from.
They couldn't keep that tremendous missile secret any
more than they could keep the Empire State Building
secret. Tourists came from miles around to take pictures of it.

The story was, its warhead was filled with flash pow-
der, and it was going to hit the moon and make a big
show. Hazel and I thought that's what the story was,
too. When it took off, we got set for a big flash on the
moon. We didn't know it was our Bud up in the warhead.
We didn't even know he was in Florida. He couldn't get
in touch with us. We thought he was up at Otis Air
Force Base on Cape Cod. That was the last place we
heard from him. And then that thing went up, right in
the middle of our view out the picture window.

You say you're superstitious sometimes, Mr. Ivankov.
Me too. Sometimes I can't help thinking it was all meant
to be right from the very first—even the way our picture window is aimed. There weren't any rockets going
up down here when we built. We moved down here from
Pittsburgh, which maybe you know is the center of our
steel industry. And we figured we maybe weren't going to
break any records for pumping gas, but at least we'd be
way far away from any bomb targets, in case there
was another war. And the next thing we know, a rocket
center goes up almost next door, and our little boy is a
man, and he goes up in a rocket and dies.

The more we think about it, the more we're sure it was
meant to be. I never got it straight in my mind about
religion in Russia. You don't mention it. Anyway, we
are religious, and we think God singled out Bud and
your boy, too, to die in a special way for a special reason. When everybody was asking, "How is it going to
end?"—well, maybe this is how God meant for it to end.
I don't see how it can keep on.

Mr. Ivankov, one thing that threw me as much as
anything was the way Mr. Koshevoi kept telling the U.N.

that Bud was a killer. He called Bud a mad dog and a gangster. I'm glad you don't feel that way, because that's the wrong way to feel about Bud. It was flying and not killing he liked. Mr. Koshevoi made a big thing out of how cultured and educated and all your boy was, and how wild and ignorant mine was. He made it sound as though a juvenile delinquent had murdered a college professor.

Bud never was in any trouble with the police, and he didn't have a cruel streak. He never went hunting, for instance, and he never drove like a crazy man, and he got drunk only one time I know of, and that was an experiment. He was proud of his reflexes, see? His health was on his mind all the time, because he had to be healthy to be a great flyer. I keep looking around for the right word for Bud, and I guess the one Hazel suggested is the best one. It sounded kind of stuffed-up to me at first, but now I'm used to it, and it sounds right. Hazel says Bud was dignified. Man and boy, that's what he was —straight and serious and polite and pretty much alone.

I think he knew he was going to die young. That one time he got drunk, just to find out what alcohol was, he talked to me more than he'd ever talked before. He was nineteen then. And then was the only time he let me know he knew death was all balled up in what he wanted to do with his life. It wasn't other people's deaths he was talking about, Mr. Ivankov. It was his own. "One nice thing about flying," he said to me that night. "What's that?" I said. "You never know how bad it is till it's too late," he said, "and when it happens, it happens so fast you never know what hit you."

That was death he was talking about, and a special dignified, honorable kind of death. You say you were in the war and had a hard time. Same here, so I guess we both know about what kind of death it was that Bud had in mind. It was a soldier's death.

We got the news he was dead three days after the big rocket went up across the water. The telegram said he had died on a secret mission, and we couldn't have any details. We had our Congressman, Earl Waterman, find out what he could about Bud. Mr. Waterman came and talked to us personally, and he looked like he had seen God. He said he couldn't tell us what Bud had done, but it was one of the most heroic things in United States history.

The word they put out on the big rocket we saw launched was that the firing was satisfactory, the knowledge gained was something wonderful, and the missile had been blown up over the ocean somewhere. That was that.

Then the word came that the man in the Russian baby moon was dead. I tell you honestly, Mr. Ivankov, that was good news to us, because that man sailing way up there with all those instruments meant just one thing, and that was a terrible weapon of war.

Then we heard the Russian baby moon had turned into a bunch of baby moons, all spreading apart. Then, this last month, the cat was out of the bag. Two of the baby moons were men. One was your boy, the other was mine.

I'm crying now, Mr. Ivankov. I hope some good comes of the death of our two boys. I guess that's what millions of fathers have hoped for as long as there have been people. There in the U.N. they're still arguing about what happened way up in the sky. I'm glad they've got around to where everybody, including your Mr. Koshevoi, agrees it was an accident. Bud was up there to get pictures of what your boy was riding in, and to show off for the United States some. He got too close. I like to think they lived a little while after the crash, and tried to save each other.

THEY say they'll be up there for hundreds of years, long after you and I are gone. In their orbits they will meet and part and meet again, and the astronomers know exactly where their next meeting place will be. Like you say, they are up there like the sun and the moon and the stars.

I enclose a photograph of my boy in his uniform. He was twenty-one when the picture was taken. He was only twenty-two when he died. Bud was picked for that mission on account of he was the finest flyer in the United States Air Force. That's what he always wanted to be. That's what he was.

I grasp your hand.

Charles M. Ashland
Petroleum Merchant
Titusville, Florida
U. S. A.

The Euphio
Question

LADIES and gentlemen of the Federal Communication Commission, I appreciate this opportunity to testify o the subject before you.

I'm sorry—or maybe "heartsick" is the word—tha news has leaked out about it. But now that word i getting around and coming to your official notice, I migh as well tell the story straight and pray to God that I ca convince you that America doesn't want what we di covered.

I won't deny that all three of us—Lew Harrison, th radio announcer; Dr. Fred Bockman, the physicist; an myself, a sociology professor—all found peace of mind We did. And I won't say it's wrong for people to see peace of mind. But if somebody thinks he wants peace mind the way we found it, he'd be well advised to see coronary thrombosis instead.

Lew, Fred and I found peace of mind by sitting in eas chairs and turning on a gadget the size of a table-mod television set. No herbs, no golden rule, no muscle co trol, no sticking our noses in other people's troubles to forget our own; no hobbies, Taoism, push-ups or contemplation of a lotus. The gadget is, I think, what a lot of people vaguely foresaw as the crowning achievement of civilization: an electronic something-or-other, cheap, easily mass-produced, that can, at the flick of a switch, provide tranquillity. I see you have one here.

My first brush with synthetic peace of mind was six months ago. It was also then that I got to know Lew Harrison, I'm sorry to say. Lew is chief announcer of our town's only radio station. He makes his living with his loud mouth, and I'd be surprised if it were anyone but he who brought this matter to your attention.

Lew has, along with about thirty other shows, a weekly science program. Every week he gets some professor from Wyandotte College and interviews him about his particular field. Well, six months ago Lew worked up a program around a young dreamer and faculty friend of mine, Dr. Fred Bockman. I gave Fred a lift to the radio station, and he invited me to come on in and watch. For the heck of it, I did.

Fred Bockman is thirty and looks eighteen. Life has left no marks on him, because he hasn't paid much attention to it. What he pays most of his attention to, and what Lew Harrison wanted to interview him about, is this eight-ton umbrella of his that he listens to the stars with. It's a big radio antenna rigged up on a telescope mount. The way I understand it, instead of looking at the stars through a telescope, he aims this thing out in space and picks up radio signals coming from different heavenly bodies.

Of course, there aren't people running radio stations out there. It's just that many of the heavenly bodies pour out a lot of energy and some of it can be picked up in the radio-frequency band. One good thing Fred's rig does is to spot stars hidden from telescopes by big clouds of cosmic dust. Radio signals from them get through the clouds to Fred's antenna.

That isn't all the outfit can do, and, in his interview with Fred, Lew Harrison saved the most exciting part until the end of the program. "That's very interesting, Dr. Bockman," Lew said. "Tell me, has your radio telescope turned up anything else about the universe that hasn't been revealed by ordinary light telescopes?"

This was the hooker. "Yes, it has," Fred said. "We've found about fifty spots in space, *not hidden by cosmic dust,* that give off powerful radio signals. Yet no heavenly bodies at all seem to be there."

"Well!" Lew said in mock surprise. "I should say that *is* something! Ladies and gentlemen, for the first time in radio history, we bring you the noise from Dr. Bockman's mysterious voids." They had strung a line out to Fred's antenna on the campus. Lew waved to the engineer to switch in the signals coming from it. "Ladies and gentlemen, the voice of nothingness!"

The noise wasn't much to hear—a wavering hiss, more like a leaking tire than anything else. It was supposed to be on the air for five seconds. When the engineer switched it off, Fred and I were inexplicably grinning like idiots. I felt relaxed and tingling. Lew Harrison looked as though he'd stumbled into the dressing room at the Copacabana. He glanced at the studio clock, appalled. The monotonous hiss had been on the air for five minutes! If the engineer's cuff hadn't accidentally caught on the switch, it might be on yet.

Fred laughed nervously, and Lew hunted for his place in the script. "The hiss from nowhere," Lew said. "Dr. Bockman, has anyone proposed a name for these interesting voids?"

"No," Fred said. "At the present time they have neither a name nor an explanation."

The voids the hiss came from have still to be explained, but I've suggested a name for them that shows signs of sticking: "Bockman's Euphoria." We may not know what the spots are, but we know what they do, so the name's a good one. Euphoria, since it means a sense of buoyancy and well-being, is really the only word that will do.

AFTER the broadcast, Fred, Lew and I were cordial to one another to the point of being maudlin.

"I can't remember when a broadcast has been such a pleasure," Lew said. Sincerity is not his forte, yet he meant it.

"It's been one of the most memorable experiences of my life," Fred said, looking puzzled. "Extraordinarily pleasant."

We were all embarrassed by the emotion we felt, and parted company in bafflement and haste. I hurried home for a drink, only to walk into the middle of another unsettling experience.

The house was quiet, and I made two trips through it before discovering that I was not alone. My wife, Susan, a good and lovable woman who prides herself on feeding her family well and on time, was lying on the couch, staring dreamily at the ceiling. "Honey," I said tentatively, "I'm home. It's suppertime."

"Fred Bockman was on the radio today," she said in a faraway voice.

"I know. I was with him in the studio."

"He was out of this world," she sighed. "Simply out of this world. That noise from space—when he turned that on, everything just seemed to drop away from me. I've been lying here, just trying to get over it."

"Uh-huh," I said, biting my lip. "Well, guess I'd better round up Eddie." Eddie is my ten-year-old son, and captain of an apparently invincible neighborhood baseball team.

"Save your strength, Pop," said a small voice from the shadows.

"You home? What's the matter? Game called off on account of atomic attack?"

"Nope. We finished eight innings."

"Beating 'em so bad they didn't want to go on, eh?"

"Oh, they were doing pretty good. Score was tied, and they had two men on and two outs." He talked as though he were recounting a dream. "And then," he said, his eyes widening, "everybody kind of lost interest, just wandered off. I came home and found the old lady curled up here, so I lay down on the floor."

"Why?" I asked incredulously.

"Pop," Eddie said thoughtfully, "I'm damned if I know."

"Eddie!" his mother said.

"Mom," Eddie said, "I'm damned if you know either."

I was damned if anybody could explain it, but I had a nagging hunch. I dialed Fred Bockman's number. "Fred, am I getting you up from dinner?"

"I wish you were," Fred said. "Not a scrap to eat in the house, and I let Marion have the car today so she could do the marketing. Now she's trying to find a grocery open."

"Couldn't get the car started, eh?"

"Sure she got the car started," said Fred. "She even

got to the market. Then she felt so good she walked right out of the place again." Fred sounded depressed. "I guess it's a woman's privilege to change her mind, but it's the lying that hurts."

"Marion lied? I don't believe it."

"She tried to tell me everybody wandered out of the market with her—clerks and all."

"Fred," I said, "I've got news for you. Can I drive out right after supper?"

When I arrived at Fred Bockman's farm, he was staring, dumbfounded, at the evening paper.

"The whole town went nuts!" Fred said. "For no reason at all, all the cars pulled up to the curb like there was a hook and ladder going by. Says here people shut up in the middle of sentences and stayed that way for five minutes. Hundreds wandered around in the cold in their shirt sleeves, grinning like tooth-paste ads." He rattled the paper. "This *is* what you wanted to talk to me about?"

I nodded. "It all happened when that noise was being broadcast, and I thought maybe—"

"The odds are about one in a million that there's any maybe about it," said Fred. "The time checks to the second."

"But most people weren't listening to the program."

"They didn't have to listen, if my theory's right. We took those faint signals from space, amplified them about a thousand times, and rebroadcast them. Anybody within reach of the transmitter would get a good dose of the stepped-up radiations, whether he wanted to or not." He shrugged. "Apparently that's like walking past a field of burning marijuana."

"How come you never felt the effect at work?"

"Because I never amplified and rebroadcast the signals. The radio station's transmitter is what really put the sock into them."

"So what're you going to do next?"

Fred looked surprised. "Do? What is there to do but report it in some suitable journal?"

WITHOUT a preliminary knock, the front door burst open and Lew Harrison, florid and panting, swept into the room and removed his great polo coat with a bull-fighterlike flourish. "You're cutting him in on it, too?" he demanded, pointing at me.

Fred blinked at him. "In on what?"

"The millions," Lew said. "The billions."

"Wonderful," Fred said. "What are you talking about?"

"The noise from the stars!" Lew said "They love it. It drives 'em nuts. Didja see the papers?" He sobered for an instant. "It *was* the noise that did it, wasn't it Doc?"

"We think so," Fred said. He looked worried. "How, exactly, do you propose we get our hands on these millions or billions?"

"Real estate!" Lew said raptly. " 'Lew,' I said to myself, 'Lew, how can you cash in on this gimmick if you can't get a monopoly on the universe? And, Lew,' I asked myself 'how can you sell the stuff when anybody can get it free while you're broadcasting it?' "

"Maybe it's the kind of thing that shouldn't be cashed in on," I suggested uneasily. "I mean, we don't know a great deal about—"

"Is happiness bad?" Lew interrupted hotly.

"No," I admitted.

"Okay, and what we'd do with this stuff from the stars is make people happy. Now I suppose you're going to tell me that's bad?"

"People ought to be happy," Fred said.

"Okay, okay," Lew said loftily. "That's what we're going to do for the people. And the way the people can show their gratitude is in real estate." He looked out the window. "Good—a barn. We can start right there. We set up a transmitter in the barn, run a line out to your antenna, Doc, and we've got a real-estate development."

"Sorry," Fred said. "I don't follow you. This place wouldn't do for a development. The roads are poor, no bus service or shopping center, the view is lousy and the ground is full of rocks."

Lew nudged Fred several times with his elbow. "Doc, Doc, Doc—sure it's got drawbacks, but with that transmitter in the barn, you can give them the most precious thing in all creation—happiness."

"Euphoria Heights," I said.

"That's great!" said Lew. "I'd get the prospects, Doc, and you'd sit up there in the barn with your hand on the switch. Once a prospect set foot on Euphoria Heights, and you shot the happiness to him, there's nothing he wouldn't pay for a lot."

"Every house a home, as long as the power doesn't fail," I said.

"Then," Lew said, his eyes shining, "when we sell all the lots here, we move the transmitter and start another development. Maybe we'd get a fleet of transmitters going." He snapped his fingers. "Sure! Mount 'em on wheels."

"I somehow don't think the police would think highly of us," Fred said.

"Okay, so when they come to investigate, you throw the old switch and give *them* a jolt of happiness." He shrugged. "Hell, I might even get bighearted and let them have a corner lot."

"No," Fred said quietly. "If I ever joined a church, I couldn't face the minister."

"So we give *him* a jolt," Lew said brightly.

"No," Fred said. "Sorry."

"Okay," Lew said, rising and pacing the floor. "I was prepared for that. I've got an alternative, and this one's strictly legitimate. We'll make a little amplifier with a transmitter and an aerial on it. Shouldn't cost over fifty bucks to make, so we'd price it in the range of the common man—five hundred bucks, say. We make arrangements with the phone company to pipe signals from your antenna right into the homes of people with these sets. The sets take the signal from the phone line, amplify it and broadcast it through the houses to make everybody in them happy. See? Instead of turning on the radio or television, everybody's going to want to turn on the happiness. No casts, no stage sets, no expensive cameras—no nothing but that hiss."

"We could call it the euphoriaphone," I suggested, "or 'euphio' for short."

"That's great, that's great!" Lew said. "What do you say, Doc?"

"I don't know." Fred looked worried. "This sort of thing is out of my line."

"We all have to recognize our limitations, Doc," Lew said expansively. "I'll handle the business end, and you handle the technical end." He made a motion as though to put on his coat. "Or maybe you don't want to be a millionaire?"

"Oh, yes, yes indeed I do," Fred said quickly. "Yes indeed."

"All righty," Lew said, dusting his palms, "the first

thing we've gotta do is build one of the sets and test her."

This part of it *was* down Fred's alley, and I could could see the problem interested him. "It's really a pretty simple gadget," he said. "I suppose we could throw one together and run a test out here next week."

THE first test of the euphoriaphone, or euphio, took place in Fred Bockman's living room on a Saturday afternoon, five days after Fred's and Lew's sensational radio broadcast.

There were six guinea pigs—Lew, Fred and his wife Marion, myself, my wife Susan and my son Eddie. The Bockmans had arranged chairs in a circle around a card table, on which rested a gray steel box.

Protruding from the box was a long buggy whip of an aerial that scraped the ceiling. While Fred fussed with the box, the rest of us made nervous small talk over sandwiches and beer. Eddie, of course, wasn't drinking beer, though he was badly in need of a sedative. He was annoyed at having been brought out to the farm instead of taken to a ball game, and was threatening to take it out on the Bockmans' Early American furnishings. He was playing a spirited game of flies and grounders with himself near the French doors, using a dead tennis ball, and a poker for a bat.

"Eddie," Susan said for the tenth time, "please stop."

"It's under control, under control," Eddie said disdainfully, playing the ball off four walls and catching it with one hand.

Marion, who vents her maternal instincts on her immaculate furnishings, couldn't hide her distress at Eddie's turning the place into a gymnasium. Lew, in his way, was trying to calm her. "Let him wreck the dump," Lew said. "You'll be moving into a palace one of these days."

"It's ready," Fred said softly.

We looked at him with surprise, uneasiness. Fred plugged two jacks from the phone line into the gray box. This was the direct line to his antenna on the campus, and clockwork would keep the antenna fixed on one of the mysterious voids in the sky—the most potent of Bockman's Euphoria. He plugged a cord from the box into an electrical outlet in the baseboard, and rested his hand on a switch. "Ready?"

"Don't, Fred!" I said. Suddenly I was scared stiff.

"Turn it on, turn it on," Lew said. "We wouldn't have the telephone today if Bell hadn't had the guts to call somebody up."

"I'll stand right here by the switch, ready to flick her off if something goes sour," Fred said reassuringly. There was a click, a hum, and the euphio was on.

A deep, unanimous sigh filled the room. The poker slipped from Eddie's hands. He moved across the room in a stately sort of waltz, knelt by his mother and laid his head in her lap. Fred drifted away from his post, humming, his eyes half closed.

Lew Harrison was the first to speak, continuing his conversation with Marion. "But who cares for material wealth?" he asked earnestly. He turned to Susan for confirmation.

"Uh-uh," said Susan, shaking her head dreamily. She put her arms around Lew, and kissed him for about five minutes.

"Say," I said, patting Susan on the back, "you kids get along swell, don't you? Isn't that nice, Fred?"

"Eddie," Marion said solicitously, "I think there's a real baseball in the hall closet. A *hard* ball. Wouldn't that be more fun than that old tennis ball?" Eddie didn't stir.

Fred was still prowling around the room, smiling, his eyes now closed all the way. His heel caught in a lamp cord, and he went sprawling on the hearth, his head in the ashes. "Hi-ho, everybody," he said, his eyes still closed. "Bunged my head on an andiron." He stayed there, giggling occasionally.

"The doorbell's been ringing for a while," Susan said. "I don't suppose it means anything."

"Come in, come in," I shouted. This somehow struck everyone as terribly funny. We all laughed uproariously, including Fred, whose guffaws blew up little gray clouds from the ashpit.

A SMALL, very serious old man in white had let himself in, and was now standing in the vestibule, looking at us with alarm. "Milkman," he said uncertainly. He held out a slip of paper to Marion. "I can't read the last line in your note," he said. "What's that say about cottage cheese, cheese, cheese, cheese, cheese . . ." His voice trailed off as he settled, tailor-fashion, to the floor beside Marion. After he'd been silent for perhaps three quarters of an hour, a look of concern crossed his face. "Well," he said apathetically, "I can only stay for a minute. My truck's parked out on the shoulder, kind of blocking things." He started to stand. Lew gave the volume knob on the euphio a twist. The milkman wilted to the floor.

"Aaaaaaaaaaah," said everybody.

"Good day to be indoors," the milkman said. "Radio says we'll catch the tail end of the Atlantic hurricane."

"Let 'er come," I said. "I've got my car parked under a big, dead tree." It seemed to make sense. Nobody took exception to it. I lapsed back into a warm fog of silence and thought of nothing whatsoever. These lapses seemed to last for a matter of seconds before they were interrupted by conversation of newcomers. Looking back, I see now that the lapses were rarely less than six hours.

I was snapped out of one, I recall, by a repetition of the doorbell's ringing. "I said come in," I mumbled.

"And I did," the milkman said.

The door swung open, and a state trooper glared in at us. "Who the hell's got his milk truck out there blocking the road?" he demanded. He spotted the milkman. "Aha! Don't you know somebody could get killed, coming around a blind curve into that thing?" He yawned, and his ferocious expression gave way to an affectionate smile. "It's so damn' unlikely," he said, "I don't know why I ever brought it up." He sat down by Eddie. "Hey, kid—like guns?" He took his revolver from its holster. "Look—just like Hoppy's."

Eddie took the gun, aimed it at Marion's bottle collection and fired. A large blue bottle popped to dust and the window behind the collection splintered. Cold air roared in through the opening.

"He'll make a cop yet," Marion chortled.

"God, I'm happy," I said, feeling a little like crying. "I got the swellest little kid and the swellest bunch of friends and the swellest old wife in the world." I heard the gun go off twice more, and then dropped into heavenly oblivion.

Again the doorbell roused me. "How many times do I have to tell you—for Heaven's sake, come in," I said, without opening my eyes.

"I *did*," the milkman said.

I heard the tramping of many feet, but had no curiosity about them. A little later, I noticed that I was having difficulty breathing. Investigation revealed that I had slipped to the floor, and that several Boy Scouts had bivouacked on my chest and abdomen.

"You want something?" I asked the tenderfoot whose hot, measured breathing was in my face.

"Beaver Patrol wanted old newspapers, but forget it," he said. "We'd just have to carry 'em somewhere."

"And do your parents know where you are?"

"Oh, sure. They got worried and came after us." He jerked his thumb at several couples lined up against the baseboard, smiling into the teeth of the wind and rain lashing in at them through the broken window.

"Mom, I'm kinda hungry," Eddie said.

"Oh, Eddie—you're not going to make your mother cook just when we're having such a wonderful time," Susan said.

Lew Harrison gave the euphio's volume knob another twist. "There, kid, how's that?"

"Aaaaaaaaaaah," said everybody.

When awareness intruded on oblivion again, I felt around for the Beaver Patrol, and found them missing. I opened my eyes to see that they and Eddie and the milkman and Lew and the trooper were standing by a picture window, cheering. The wind outside was roaring and slashing savagely and driving raindrops through the broken window as though they'd been fired from air rifles. I shook Susan gently, and together we went to the window to see what might be so entertaining.

"She's going, she's going, she's going," the milkman cried ecstatically.

SUSAN and I arrived just in time to join in the cheering as a big elm crashed down on our sedan.

"Kee-*runch!*" said Susan, and I laughed until my stomach hurt.

"Get Fred," Lew said urgently. "He's gonna miss seeing the barn go!"

"H'mm?" Fred said from the fireplace.

"Aw, Fred, you missed it," Marion said.

"Now we're really gonna see something," Eddie yelled. "The power line's going to get it this time. Look at that poplar lean!"

The poplar leaned closer, closer, closer to the power

line; and then a gust brought it down in a hail of sparks and a tangle of wires. The lights in the house went off.

Now there was only the sound of the wind. "How come nobody cheered?" Lew said faintly. "The euphio—it's off!"

A horrible groan came from the fireplace. "God, I think I've got a concussion."

Marion knelt by her husband and wailed. "Darling, my poor darling—what happened to you?"

I looked at the woman I had my arms around—a dreadful, dirty old hag, with red eyes sunk deep in her head, and hair like Medusa's. "Ugh," I said, and turned away in disgust.

"Honey," wept the witch, "it's me—Susan."

Moans filled the air, and pitiful cries for food and water. Suddenly the room had become terribly cold. Only a moment before, I had imagined I was in the tropics.

"Who's got my damn' pistol?" the trooper said bleakly.

A Western Union boy I hadn't noticed before was sitting in a corner, miserably leafing through a pile of telegrams and making clucking noises.

I shuddered. "I'll bet it's Sunday morning," I said. "We've been here twelve hours!"

The Western Union boy was thunderstruck. "Sunday morning? Holy smokes! I walked in here on a Sunday night, and only saw the sun rise once." He stared around the room. "Looks like them newsreels of Buchenwald, don't it?"

The chief of the Beaver Patrol, with the incredible stamina of the young, was the hero of the day. He fell in his men in two ranks, haranguing them like an old Army top kick. While the rest of us lay draped around the room, whimpering about hunger, cold and thirst, the patrol started the furnace again, brought blankets, applied compresses to Fred's head and countless barked shins, blocked off the broken window, and made buckets of cocoa and coffee.

WITHIN two hours of the time that the power and the euphio went off, the house was warm and we had eaten. The serious respiratory cases—the parents who had sat near the broken window for twenty-four hours—had been pumped full of penicillin and hauled off to the hospital. The milkman, the Western Union boy and the trooper had refused treatment and gone home. The Beaver Patrol had saluted smartly and left. Outside, repairmen were working on the power line. Only the original group remained—Lew, Fred and Marion, Susan and myself, and Eddie. Fred, it turned out, had some pretty important-looking contusions and abrasions, but no concussion.

Susan had fallen asleep right after eating. Now she stirred. "What happened?"

"Happiness," I told her. "Incomparable, continuous happiness—happiness by the kilowatt."

Lew Harrison, who looked like an anarchist with his red eyes and fierce black beard, had been writing furiously in one corner of the room. "That's good—happiness by the kilowatt," he said. "Buy your happiness the way you buy light."

"Contract happiness the way you contract influenza," Fred said. He sneezed.

Lew ignored him. "It's a campaign, see? The first ad is for the long-hairs: 'The price of one book, which may be a disappointment, will buy you sixty hours of euphio. Euphio never disappoints.' Then we'd hit the middle class with the next one—"

"In the groin?" Fred said.

"What's the matter with you people?" Lew said. "You act as though the experiment had failed."

"Pneumonia and malnutrition are what we'd hoped for?" Marion said.

"We had a cross section of America in this room, and we made every last person happy," Lew said. "Not for just an hour, not for just a day, but for two days without a break." He arose reverently from his chair. "So what we do to keep it from killing the euphio fans is to have the thing turned on and off with clockwork, see? The owner sets it so it'll go on just as he comes home from work, then it'll go off again while he eats supper; then it goes on after supper, off again when it's bedtime; on again after breakfast, off when it's time to go to work, then on again for the wife and kids."

He ran his hands through his hair and rolled his eyes. "And the selling points—my God, the selling points! No expensive toys for the kids. For the price of a trip to the movies, people can buy thirty hours of euphio. For the price of a fifth of whisky, they can buy sixty hours of euphio!"

"Or a big family bottle of potassium cyanide," Fred said.

"Don't you see it?" Lew said incredulously. "It'll bring families together again, save the American home. No more fights over what TV or radio program to listen to. Euphio pleases one and all—we proved that. And there is no such thing as a dull euphio program."

A knock on the door interrupted him. A repairman stuck his head in to announce that the power would be on again in about two minutes.

"Look, Lew," Fred said, "this little monster could kill civilization in less time than it took to burn down Rome. We're not going into the mind-numbing business, and that's that."

"You're kidding!" Lew said, aghast. He turned to Marion. "Don't you want your husband to make a million?"

"Not by operating an electronic opium den," Marion said coldly.

Lew slapped his forehead. "It's what the public wants. This is like Louis Pasteur refusing to pasteurize milk."

"It'll be good to have the electricity again," Marion said, changing the subject. "Lights, hot-water heater, the pump, the—oh, Lord!"

The lights came on the instant she said it, but Fred and I were already in mid-air, descending on the gray box. We crashed down on it together. The card table buckled, and the plug was jerked from the wall socket. The euphio's tubes glowed red for a moment, then died.

Expressionlessly, Fred took a screwdriver from his pocket and removed the top of the box.

"Would you enjoy doing battle with progress?" he said, offering me the poker Eddie had dropped.

In a frenzy, I stabbed and smashed at the euphio's glass and wire vitals. With my left hand, and with Fred's help, I kept Lew from throwing himself between the poker and the works.

"I thought you were on my side," Lew said.

"If you breathe one word about euphio to anyone," I said, "what I just did to euphio I will gladly do to you."

AND there, ladies and gentlemen of the Federal Communications Commission, I thought the matter had ended. It deserved to end there. Now, through the medium of Lew Harrison's big mouth, word has leaked out. He has petitioned you for permission to start commercial exploitation of euphio. He and his backers have built a radio-telescope of their own.

Let me say again that all of Lew's claims are true. Euphio will do everything he says it will. The happiness it gives is perfect and unflagging in the face of incredible adversity. Near tragedies, such as the first experiment, can no doubt be avoided with clockwork to turn the sets on and off. I see that this set on the table before you is, in fact, equipped with clockwork.

The question is not whether euphio works. It does. The question is, rather, whether or not America is to enter a new and distressing phase of history where men no longer pursue happiness but buy it. This is no time for oblivion to become a national craze. The only benefit we could get from euphio would be if we could somehow lay down a peace-of-mind barrage on our enemies while protecting our own people from it.

In closing, I'd like to point out that Lew Harrison, the would-be czar of euphio, is an unscrupulous person, unworthy of public trust. It wouldn't surprise me, for instance, if he had set the clockwork on this sample euphio set so that its radiations would addle your judgments when you are trying to make a decision. In fact, it seems to be whirring suspiciously at this very moment, and I'm so happy I could cry. I've got the swellest little kid and the swellest bunch of friends and the swellest old wife in the world. And good old Lew Harrison is the salt of the earth, believe me. I sure wish him a lot of good luck with his new enterprise.

More Stately Mansions

WE'VE known the McClellans, Grace and George, for about two years now. They were the first neighbors to call on us and welcome us to the village.

I expected that initial conversation to lag uncomfortably after the first pleasantries, but not at all. Grace, her eyes quick and bright as a sparrow's, found subject matter enough to keep her talking for hours.

"You know," she said excitedly, "your living room could be a perfect dream! Couldn't it, George? Can't you see it?"

"Yup," said her husband. "Nice, all right."

"Just tear out all this white-painted woodwork," Grace said, her eyes narrowing. "Panel it all in knotty pine wiped with linseed oil with a little umber added. Cover the couch in lipstick red—*red* red. Know what I mean?"

"Red?" said Anne, my wife.

"Red! Don't be afraid of color."

"I'll try not to be," Anne said.

"And just cover the whole wall there, those two ugly

little windows and all, with bottle-green curtains. Can't you see it? It'd be almost exactly like that problem living room in the February *Better House and Garden*. You remember that, of course."

"I must have missed that," said Anne. The month was August.

"Or was it *Good Homelife,* George?" Grace said.

"Don't remember offhand," said George.

"Well, I can look it up in my files and put my hand right on it." Grace stood up suddenly, and, uninvited, started a tour through the rest of the house.

She went from room to room, consigning a piece of furniture to the Salvation Army, detecting a fraudulent antique, shrugging partitions out of existence, and pacing off a chartreuse, wall-to-wall carpet we would have to order before we did another thing. "Start with the carpet," she said firmly, "and build from there. It'll pull your whole downstairs together if you build from the carpet."

"Um," said Anne.

"I hope you saw Nineteen Basic Carpet Errors in the June *Home Beautiful*."

"Oh yes, yes indeed," Anne said.

"Good. Then I don't have to tell you how wrong you can go, *not* building from the carpet. George—Oh, he's still in the living room."

I caught a glimpse of George on the living-room couch, lost in his own thoughts. He straightened up and smiled.

I followed Grace, trying to change the subject. "Let's see, you are on our north side. Who's to our south?"

Grace held up her hands. "Oh! You haven't met them —the Jenkinses. George," she called, "they want to know about the Jenkinses." From her voice, I gathered that our southerly neighbors were sort of lovable beachcombers.

"Now, Grace, they're nice enough people," George said.

"Oooh, George," Grace said, "you know how the Jenkinses are. Yes, they're nice, but . . ." She laughed and shook her head.

"But what?" I said. The possibilities raced through my mind. Nudists? Heroin addicts? Anarchists? Hamster raisers?

"In 1945 they moved in," Grace said, "and right off the bat they bought two beautiful Hitchcock chairs, and . . ." This time she sighed and shrugged.

"And what?" I demanded. And spilled India ink on them? And found a bundle of thousand-dollar bills rolled up in a hollow leg?

"And that's all," Grace said. "They just stopped right there."

"How's that?" said Anne.

"Don't you see? They started out beautifully with those two chairs; then they just petered out."

"Oh," said Anne slowly. "I see—a flash in the pan. So *that's* what's wrong with the Jenkinses. Aha!"

"Fie on the Jenkinses," I said.

Grace didn't hear me. She was patrolling between the living room and dining room, and I noticed that every time she entered or left the living room, she made a jog in her course, always at exactly the same place. Curious, I went over to the spot she avoided, and bounced up and down a couple of times to see if the floor was unsound at that point, or what.

In she came again, and she looked at me with surprise. "Oh!"

"Did I do something wrong?" I asked.

"I just didn't expect to find *you* there."

"Sorry."

"That's where the cobbler's bench goes, you know."

I stepped aside, and watched uncomfortably as she bent over the phantom cobbler's bench. I think it was then that she first alarmed me, made me feel a little less like laughing.

"With one or two little nail drawers open, and ivy growing out of them," she explained. "Cute?" She stepped around it, being careful not to bark her shins, and went up the stairs to the second floor. "Do you mind if I have a look around up here?" she asked gaily.

"Go right ahead," said Anne.

George had gotten up off the sofa. He stood looking up the stairs for a minute; then he held up his empty highball glass. "Mind if I have another?"

"Say, I'm sorry, George. We haven't been taking very good care of you. You bet. Help yourself. The bottle's there in the dining room."

He went straight to it, and poured himself a good inch and a half of whisky in the bottom of the tumbler.

"The tile in this bathroom is all wrong for your towels, of course," Grace said from upstairs.

Anne, who had padded after her like a housemaid, agreed bleakly. "Of course."

George lifted his glass, winked, and drained it. "Don't let her throw you," he said. "Just her way of talking. Got a damn' nice house here. *I* like it, and so does she."

"Thanks, George. That's nice of you."

ANNE and Grace came downstairs again, Anne looking quite bushed. "Oh, you men!" Grace said. "You just think we're silly, don't you?" She smiled companionably at Anne. "They just don't understand what interests women. What were you two talking about while we were having such a good time?"

"I was telling him he ought to wallpaper his trees and make chintz curtains for his keyholes," George said playfully.

"Mmmmm," said Grace. "Well, time to go home, dear."

She paused outside the front door. "Nice basic lines to this door," she said. "That gingerbread will come right off, if you get a chisel under it. And you can lighten it by rubbing on white paint, then rubbing it off again right away. It'll look more like *you*."

"You've been awfully helpful," said Anne.

"Well, it's a dandy house the way it is," George said.

"I swear," Grace said, "I'll never understand how so many artists are men. No man I ever met had a grain of artistic temperament in him."

"Bushwa," said George quietly. And then he surprised me. The glance he gave Grace was affectionate and possessive.

"It *is* a dull little dump, I guess," said Anne gloomily, after the McClellans had left.

"Oh, listen—it's a swell house."

"I guess. But it needs so much done to it. I didn't realize. Golly, their place must be something. They've been in it for five years, she said. You can imagine what she could do to a place in five years—everything right, right down to the last nailhead."

"It isn't much from the outside. Anyway, Anne, this isn't like you."

She shook her head, as though to wake herself up. "It isn't, is it? Never in my life have I had the slightest interest in keeping up with the neighbors. But there's something about that woman."

"To hell with her! Let's throw in our lot with the Jenkinses."

Anne laughed. Grace's spell was wearing off. "Are you mad? Be friends with those two-chair people, those quitters?"

"Well, we'd make our friendship contingent on their getting a new couch to go with the chairs."

"And not any couch, but the *right* couch."

"If they want to be friends of ours, they mustn't be afraid of color, and they'd better build from the carpet."

"That goes without saying," said Anne crisply.

BUT it was a long time before we found leisure for more than a nod at the Jenkinses. Grace McClellan spent most of her waking hours at our house. Almost every morning, as I was leaving for work, she would stagger into our house under a load of home magazines and insist that Anne pore over them with her in search of just the right solutions for our particular problem house.

"They must be awfully rich," Anne said at dinner one night.

"I don't think so," I said. "George has a little leather-goods store that you hardly ever see anybody in."

"Well, then every cent must go into the house."

"That I can believe. But what makes you think they're rich?"

"To hear that woman talk, you'd think money was nothing! Without batting an eyelash, she talks about ten-dollar-a-yard floor-to-ceiling draperies, says fixing up the kitchen shouldn't cost more than a lousy fifteen hundred dollars—without the fieldstone fireplace, of course."

"What's a kitchen without a fieldstone fireplace?"

"And a circular couch."

"Isn't there some way you can keep her away, Anne? She's wearing you out. Can't you just tell her you're too busy to see her?"

"I haven't the heart, she's so kind and friendly and lonely," said Anne helplessly. "Besides, there's no getting through to her. She doesn't hear what I say. Her head is just crammed full of blueprints, cloth, furniture, wallpaper and paint."

"Change the subject."

"Change the course of the Mississippi! Talk about politics, and she talks about remodeling the White House; talk about dogs, and she talks about doghouses."

The telephone rang, and I answered it. It was Grace McClellan. "Yes, Grace?"

"You're in the office-furniture business, aren't you?"

"That's right."

"Do you ever get old filing cabinets in trade?"

"Yes. I don't like to, but sometimes I have to take them."

"Could you let me have one?"

I thought a minute. I had an old wooden wreck I was about to haul to the dump. I told her about it.

"Oh, that'll be divine! There's an article in last month's *Better House* about what to do with old filing cabinets. You can make them just darling by wallpapering them, then putting a coat of clear shellac over the paper. Can't you just see it?"

"Yep. Darling, all right. I'll bring it out tomorrow night."

"That's awfully nice of you. I wonder if you and Anne couldn't drop in for a drink then."

I accepted and hung up. "Well, the time has come," I said. "Marie Antoinette has finally invited us to have a look at Versailles."

"I'm afraid," Anne said. "It's going to make our home look so sad."

"There's more to life than decorating."

"I know, I know. I just wish you'd stay home in the daytime and keep telling me that while she's here."

The next evening, I drove the pickup truck home instead of my car, so I could deliver the old filing cabinet to Grace. Anne was already inside the McClellan house, and George came out to give me a hand.

The cabinet was an old-fashioned oak monster, and, with all the sweating and grunting, I didn't really pay much attention to the house until we'd put down our burden in the front hall.

THE first thing I noticed was that there were already two dilapidated filing cabinets in the hall, ungraced by wallpaper or clear shellac. I looked into the living room. Anne was sitting on the couch with a queer smile on her face. The couch springs had burst through the bottom and were resting nakedly on the floor. The chief illumination came from a single light bulb in a cob-webbed chandelier with sockets for six. An electric extension cord, patched with friction tape, hung from another of the sockets and led to an iron on an ironing board in the middle of the living room.

A small throw rug, the type generally seen in bathrooms, was the only floor covering, and the planks of the floor were scarred and dull from long neglect. Dust and cobwebs were everywhere, and the windows were dirty. The only sign of order or opulence was on the coffee table, where dozens of fat, slick decoration magazines were spread out like a fan.

George was nervous and more taciturn than usual, and I gathered that he was uneasy about having us in. After mixing us drinks, he sat down and maintained a fidgeting silence.

Not so with Grace. She was at a high pitch of excitement, and, seemingly, full of irrepressible pride. Sitting, rising, and sitting again a dozen times a minute, she did a sort of ballet about the room, describing exactly the way she was going to do the room over. She rubbed imaginary fabrics between her fingers, stretched out luxuriantly in a wicker chair that would one day be a plum-colored chaise longue, held her hands as far apart as she could reach to indicate the span of a limed-oak television-radio-phonograph console that was to stand against one wall.

She clapped her hands and closed her eyes. "Can you see it? Can you *see* it?"

"Simply lovely," said Anne.

"And every night, just as George is coming up the walk, I'll have Martinis ready in a frosty pewter pitcher, and I'll have a record playing on the phonograph." Grace knelt before the thin air where the console would be, selected a record from nothingness, put in on the imaginary turntable, pressed a nonexistent button, and retired to the wicker chair. To my dismay, she began to rock her head back and forth in time to the phantom music.

After a minute of this, George seemed disturbed, too. "Grace! You're going to sleep." He tried to make his tone light, but real concern showed through.

Grace shook her head and opened her eyes lazily. "I wasn't sleeping; I was listening."

"It will certainly be a charming room," Anne said, looking worriedly at me.

Grace was suddenly on her feet again, charged with new energy. "And the dining room!" Impatiently, she picked up a magazine and thumbed through it. "Now, wait, where is it, where is it? No, not that one." She let the magazine drop. "Oh, of course, I clipped it last night and put it in the files. Remember, George? The dining-room table with the glass top and the place for potted flowers underneath?"

"Uh-huh."

"*That's* what goes in the dining room," Grace said happily. "See? You look right through the table, and there, underneath, are geraniums, African violets or anything you want to put there. Fun?" She hurried to the filing cabinets. "You've got to see it in color, really."

Anne and I followed her politely, and waited while she ran her finger along the dividers in the drawers. The drawers, I saw, were jammed with cloth and wallpaper samples, paint color cards, and pages taken from magazines. She had already filled two cabinets, and was ready to overflow into the third, the one I'd brought. The drawers were labeled, simply, "Living room," "Kitchen," "Dining room," and so on.

"Quite a filing system," I said to George, who was just brushing by with a fresh drink in his hand.

He looked at me closely, as though he was trying to make up his mind whether I was kidding him or not. "It is," he said at last. "There's even a section about the workshop she wants me to have in the basement." He sighed. "Someday."

Grace held up a little square of transparent blue plastic. "And this is the material for the kitchen curtains, over the sink and automatic dishwasher. Waterproof, and it wipes clean."

"It's darling," Anne said. "You have an automatic dishwasher?"

"Mmmmm?" Grace said, smiling at some distant horizon. "Oh—dishwasher? No, but I know exactly the one we want. We've made up our minds on that, haven't we, George?"

"Yes, dear."

"And someday . . ." said Grace happily, running her fingers over the contents of a file drawer.

"Someday . . ." said George.

As I say, two years have passed since then, since we first met the McClellans. Anne, with compassion and tenderness, invented harmless ways of keeping Grace from spending all her time at our house with her magazines. But we formed a neighborly habit of having a drink with the McClellans once or twice a month.

I liked George, and he grew friendly and talkative when he'd made sure we weren't going to bait his wife about interior decorating, something almost everyone else in the neighborhood was fond of doing. He adored Grace, and made light of her preoccupation, as he had done at our first meeting, only when he didn't know the people before whom she was performing. Among friends, he did nothing to discourage or disparage her dreaming.

Anne bore the brunt of Grace's one-track conversations as sort of a Christian service, listening with tact and patience. George and I ignored them, and had a pleasant enough time talking about everything but interior decoration.

In these talks it came out bit by bit that George had been in a bad financial jam for years, and that things refused to get better. The "someday" that Grace had been planning for for five years, George said, seemed to recede another month as each new home magazine appeared on the newsstands. It was this, I decided, not Grace, that kept him drinking more than his share.

And the filing cabinets got fuller and fuller, and the McClellan house got dowdier and dowdier. But not once did Grace's excitement about what their house was going to be like flag. If anything, it increased, and time and again we would have to follow her about the house to hear just how it was all going to be.

And then a fairly sad thing and an awfully nice thing happened to the McClellans. The sad thing was that Grace came down with a virus infection that kept her in the hospital two months. The nice thing was that George inherited a little money from a relative he'd never met.

While Grace was in the hospital, George often had supper with us; and the day he received his legacy, his taciturnity dropped away completely. To our surprise, *he* now talked interior decoration with fervor and to the exclusion of everything else.

"You've got the bug too, now," Anne said, laughing.

"Bug, hell! I've got the money! I'm going to surprise Grace by having that house just the way she wants it, when she comes home."

"Exactly, George?"

"Eggs-zactly!"

And Anne and I were willingly drafted to help him. We went through Grace's files and found detailed specifications for every room, right down to book ends and soap dishes. It was a tough job tracking down every item, but George was indefatigable, and so was Anne, and money was no object.

Time was everything, money was nothing. Electricians, plasterers, masons and carpenters worked around the clock for bonus wages; and Anne, for no pay at all, harassed department stores into hurrying with the houseful of furniture she'd ordered.

Two days before Grace was to come home, the inheritance was gone, and the house was magnificent. George was unquestionably the happiest, proudest man on earth. The job was flawless, save for one tiny detail not worth mentioning. Anne had failed to match exactly the yellow square of cloth Grace had wanted for her living-room curtains and the cover for the couch. The shade Anne had had to settle for was just a little bit lighter. George and I couldn't see the difference at all.

And then Grace came home, cheerful but weak, leaning on George's arm. It was late in the afternoon, and Anne and I were waiting in the living room, literally trembling with excitement. As George helped Grace up the walk, Anne fussed nervously with a bouquet of red roses she had brought and placed in a massive glass vase in the center of the coffee table.

We heard George's hand on the latch, the door swung open, and the McClellans stood on the threshold of their dream house.

"Oh, George," Grace murmured. She let go of his arm, and, as though miraculously drawing strength from her surroundings, she walked from room to room, looking all about her as we had seen her do a thousand times. But this time of times she was speechless.

She returned at last to the living room, and sank onto the plum-colored chaise longue.

George turned down the volume of the phonograph to a sweet whisper. "Well?"

Grace sighed. "Don't rush me," she said. "I'm trying to find the words, the exact words."

"You like it?" George asked.

Grace looked at him and laughed incredulously. "Oh, George, George, of course I like it! You darling, it's wonderful! I'm home, home at last." Her lip trembled, and we all began to cloud up.

"Nothing wrong?" George asked huskily.

"You've taken wonderful care of it. Everything's so clean and beautiful."

"Well, it'd sure be a surprise if things *weren't* clean," George said. He clapped his hands together. "Now then, you well enough for a drink?"

"I'm not dead."

"Leave us out, George," I said. "We're leaving. We just had to see her expression when she walked in, but now we'll clear out."

"Oh, say now—" George said.

"No. I mean it. We're going. You two ought to be alone—you *three,* including the house."

"Stay right where you are," George said. He hurried into the dazzling white kitchen to mix the drinks.

"All right, so we'll sneak out," Anne said. We started for the front door. "Don't get up, Grace."

"Well, if you really won't stay, good-by," Grace said from the chaise longue. "I hardly know how to thank you."

"It was the most fun I've had in years," said Anne. She looked proudly around the room, and went over to the coffee table to rearrange the roses slightly. "The only thing that worried me was the color of the slip cover and curtains. Are they all right?"

"Why, Anne, did you notice them too? I wasn't even going to mention them. It would certainly be silly to let a little thing like that spoil my homecoming." She frowned a little.

Anne was crestfallen. "Oh dear, I hope they didn't spoil it."

"No, no, of course they didn't," Grace said. "I don't quite understand it, but it doesn't matter a bit."

"Well, I can explain," Anne said.

"Something in the air, I suppose."

"In the air?" Anne said.

"Well, how else can you explain it? That material held its color just perfectly for years, and then, poof, it fades like this in a few weeks."

George walked in with a frosty pewter pitcher. "Now, you'll stay for a quick one, won't you?"

Anne and I took glasses hungrily, gratefully, wordlessly.

"There's a new *Home Beautiful* that came today, sweetheart," George said.

Grace shrugged. "Read one and you've read them all." She lifted her glass. "Happy days, and thanks, darlings, so much for the roses."

The Foster
Portfolio

I'M a salesman of good advice for rich people. I'm a contact man for an investment counseling firm. It's a living, but not a whale of a one—or at least not now, when I'm just starting out. To qualify for the job, I had to buy a Homburg, a navy-blue overcoat; a double-breasted banker's gray suit, black shoes, a regimental-stripe tie, half a dozen white shirts, half a dozen pairs of black socks and gray gloves.

When I call on a client, I come by cab, and I am sleek and clean and foursquare. I carry myself as though I've made a quiet killing on the stock market, and have come to call more as a public service than anything else. When I arrive in clean wool, with crackling certificates and confidential stock analyses in crisp Manila folders, the reaction—ideally and usually—is the same accorded a minister or physician. I am in charge, and everything is going to be just fine.

I deal mostly with old ladies—the meek, who by dint of cast-iron constitutions have inherited sizable portions of the earth. I thumb through the clients' lists of securities, and relay our experts' suggestions for ways of making their portfolios—or bonanzas or piles—thrive and increase. I can speak of tens of thousands of dollars without a catch in my throat, and look at a list of securities worth more than a hundred thousand with no more fuss than a judicious "Mmmmm, uh-huh."

Since *I* don't have a portfolio, my job is a little like being a hungry delivery boy for a candy store. But I never really felt that way about it until Herbert Foster asked me to have a look at his finances.

He called one evening to say a friend had recommended me, and could I come out to talk business. I washed, shaved, dusted my shoes, put on my uniform, and made my grave arrival by cab.

People in my business—and maybe people in general—have an unsavory habit of sizing up a man's house, car and suit, and estimating his annual income. Herbert Foster was thirty-five hundred a year, or I'd never seen it. Understand, I have nothing against people in moderate circumstances, other than the crucial fact that I can't make any money off them. It made me a little sore that Foster would take my time, when the most he had to play around with, I guessed, was no more than a few hundred dollars. Say it was a thousand: my take would be a dollar or two at best.

ANYWAY, there I was in the Fosters' jerry-built postwar colonial with expansion attic, the kind of house that has a prewar car in the one-car garage. They had taken up a local furniture store on its offer of three rooms of furniture, including ash trays, a humidor and pictures for the wall, all for $199.99. Hell, I was there, and I figured I might as well go through with having a look at his pathetic problem.

"Nice place you have here, Mr. Foster," I said. "And this is your charming wife?"

A skinny, shrewish-looking woman smiled up at me vacuously. She wore a faded housecoat figured with a fox-hunting scene. The print was at war with the slip cover of the chair, and I had to squint to separate her features from the clash about her. "A pleasure, Mrs. Foster," I said. She was surrounded by underwear and socks to be mended, and Herbert said her name was Alma, which seemed entirely possible.

"And this is the young master," I said. "Bright little chap. Believe he favors his father." The two-year-old wiped his grubby hands on my trousers, snuffled, and padded off toward the piano. He stationed himself at the upper end of the keyboard, and hammered on the highest note for one minute, then two, then three.

"Musical—like his father," Alma said.

"You play, do you, Mr. Foster?"

"Classical," Herbert said. I took my first good look at him. He was lightly built, with the round, freckled face and big teeth I usually associate with a show-off or wise guy. It was hard to believe that he had settled for so plain a wife, or that he could be as fond of family life as he seemed. It may have been that I only imagined a look of quiet desperation in his eyes.

"Shouldn't you be getting on to your meeting, dear?" Herbert said.

"It was called off at the last minute."

"Now, about your portfolio—" I began.

Herbert looked rattled. "How's that?"

"Your portfolio—your securities."

"Yes, well, think we'd better talk in the bedroom. It's quieter in there."

Alma put down her sewing. "What securities?"

"The bonds, dear. The government bonds."

"Now, Herbert, you're not going to cash them in."

"No, Alma, just want to talk them over."

"I see," I said tentatively. "Uh—approximately how much in government bonds?"

"Three hundred and fifty dollars," Alma said proudly.

"Well," I said, "I don't see any need for going into the bedroom to talk. My advice, and I give it free, is to hang on to your nest egg until it matures. And now, if you'll let me phone a cab—"

"Please," Herbert said, standing in the bedroom door, "there are a couple of other things I'd like to discuss."

"What?" Alma said.

"Oh, long-range investment planning." Herbert said vaguely.

"We could use a little short-range planning for next month's grocery bill."

"Please," Herbert said to me again.

I shrugged and followed him into the bedroom. He closed the door behind me. I sat on the edge of the bed and watched him open a little door in the wall, which bared the pipes servicing the bathroom. He slid his arm up into the wall, grunted, and pulled down an envelope.

"Oho," I said apathetically, "so that's where we've got the bonds, eh? Very clever. You needn't have gone to that trouble, Mr. Foster. I have an idea what government bonds look like."

"Alma," he called.

"Yes, Herbert."

"Will you start some coffee for us?"

"I don't drink coffee at night," I said.

"We have some from dinner," Alma said.

"I can't sleep if I touch it after supper," I said.

"Fresh—we want some fresh," Herbert said.

The chair springs creaked, and her reluctant footsteps faded into the kitchen.

"Here," said Herbert, putting the envelope in my lap. "I don't know anything about this business, and I guess I ought to have professional help."

All right, so I'd give the poor guy a professional talk about his three hundred and fifty dollars in government bonds. "They're the most conservative investment you can make. They haven't the growth characteristics of many securities, and the return isn't great, but they're very safe. By all means hang onto them." I stood up. "And now, if you'll let me call a cab—"

"You haven't looked at them."

I sighed, and untwisted the red string holding the envelope shut. Nothing would do but that I admire the things. The bonds and a list of securities slid into my lap. I riffled through the bonds quickly, and then read the list of securities slowly.

"Well?"

I put the list down on the faded bedspread. I composed myself. "Ummmm, uh-huh," I said. "Do you mind telling me where the securities listed here came from?"

"Grandfather left them to me two years ago. The lawyers who handled the estate have them. They sent me that list."

"Do you know what these stocks are worth?"

"They were appraised when I inherited them." He

told me the figure, and, to my bewilderment, he looked sheepish, even a little unhappy about it.

"They've gone up a little since then."

"How much?"

"On today's market—maybe they're worth seven hundred and fifty thousand dollars, Mr. Foster. Sir."

His expression didn't change. My news moved him about as much as if I'd told him it'd been a chilly winter. He raised his eyebrows as Alma's footsteps came back into the living room. "Shhhh!"

"She doesn't know?"

"Lord, no!" He seemed to have surprised himself with his vehemence. "I mean the time isn't ripe."

"If you'll let me have this list of securities, I'll have our New York office give you a complete analysis and recommendations," I whispered. "May I call you Herbert, sir?"

MY CLIENT, Herbert Foster, hadn't had a new suit in three years; he had never owned more than one pair of shoes at a time. He worried about payments on his secondhand car, and ate tuna and cheese instead of meat, because meat was too expensive. His wife made her own clothes, and those of Herbert, Jr., and the curtains and slip covers—all cut from the same bargain bolt. The Fosters were going through hell, trying to choose between new tires or retreads for the car; and television was something they had to go two doors down the street to watch. Determinedly, they kept within the small salary Herbert made as a bookkeeper for a wholesale grocery house.

God knows it's no disgrace to live that way, which is better than the way I live, but it was pretty disturbing to watch, knowing Herbert had an income, after taxes, of perhaps twenty thousand a year.

I had our securities analysts look over Foster's holdings, and report on the stocks' growth possibilities, prospective earnings, the effects of war and peace, inflation and deflation, and so on. The report ran to twenty pages, a record for any of my clients. Usually, the reports are bound in cardboard covers. Herbert's was done up in red leatherette.

It arrived at my place on a Saturday afternoon, and I called up Herbert to ask if I could bring it out. I had exciting news for him. My by-eye estimate of the values had been off, and his portfolio, as of that day, was worth close to eight hundred and fifty thousand.

"I've got the analysis and recommendations," I said, "and things look good, Mr. Foster—*very* good. You need a little diversification here and there, and maybe more emphasis on growth, but—"

"Just go ahead and do whatever needs to be done," he said.

"When could we talk about this? It's something we ought to go over together, certainly. Tonight would be fine with me."

"I work tonight."

"Overtime at the wholesale house?"

"Another job—in a restaurant. Work Friday, Saturday and Sunday nights."

I rolled my eyes. The man had maybe seventy-five dollars a day coming in from his securities, and he worked three nights a week to make ends meet! "Monday?"

"Play organ for choir practice at the church."

"Tuesday?"

"Volunteer Fire Department drill."

"Wednesday?"

"Play piano for folk dancing at the church."

"Thursday?"

"Movie night for Alma and me."

"When, then?"

"You go ahead and do whatever needs to be done."

"Don't you want to be in on what I'm doing?"

"Do I have to be?"

"I'd feel better if you were."

"All right, Tuesday noon, lunch."

"Fine with me. Maybe you'd better have a good look at this report before then, so you can have questions ready."

He sounded annoyed. "Okay, okay, okay. I'll be here tonight until nine. Drop it off before then."

"One more thing, Herbert." I'd saved the kicker for last. "I was way off about what the stocks are worth. They're now up to about eight hundred and fifty thousand dollars."

"Um."

"I said, you're about a hundred thousand dollars richer than you thought!"

"Uh-huh. Well, you just go ahead and do whatever needs to be done."

"Yes, sir." The phone was dead.

I was delayed by other business, and I didn't get out to the Fosters' until quarter of ten. Herbert was gone. Alma answered the door, and, to my surprise, she asked for the report, which I was hiding under my coat.

"Herbert said I wasn't supposed to look at it," she said, "so you don't need to worry about me peeking."

"Herbert told you about this?" I said carefully.

"Yes. He said it's confidential reports on stocks you want to sell him."

"Yes, uh-huh—well, if he said to leave it with you, here it is."

"He told me he had to promise you not to let *anybody* look at it."

"Mmm? Oh, yes, yes. Sorry, company rules."

She was a shade hostile. "I'll tell you one thing without looking at any reports, and that is he's not going to cash those bonds to buy any stocks with."

"I'd be the last one to recommend that, Mrs. Foster."

"Then why do you keep after him?"

"He may be a good customer at a later date." I looked at my hands, which I realized had become ink-stained on the earlier call. "I wonder if I might wash up?"

Reluctantly, she let me in, keeping as far away from me as the modest floor plan would permit.

As I washed up, I thought of the list of securities Herbert had taken from between the plasterboard walls. Those securities meant winters in Florida, *filet mignon* and twelve-year-old bourbon, Jaguars, silk underwear and handmade shoes, a trip around the world. . . . Name it; Herbert Foster could have it. I sighed heavily. The soap in the Foster soap dish was mottled and dingy—a dozen little chips moistened and pressed together to make a new bar.

I thanked Alma, and started to leave. On my way out, I paused by the mantel to look at a small tinted photograph. "Good picture of you," I said. A feeble effort at public relations. "I like that."

"Everybody says that. It isn't me; it's Herbert's mother."

"Amazing likeness." And it was. Herbert had mar-

ried a girl just like the girl that married dear old dad.
"And this picture is his father?"

"*My* father. We don't want a picture of *his* father."

This looked like a sore point that might prove infor-
mative. "Herbert is such a wonderful person, his father
must have been wonderful, too, eh?"

"He deserted his wife and child. That's how wonderful
he was. You'll be smart not to mention him to Herbert."

"Sorry. Everything good about Herbert comes from his
mother?"

"She was a saint. She taught Herbert to be decent and
respectable and God-fearing." Alma was a little grim
about it.

"Was she musical, too?"

"He gets that from his father. But what he does
with it is something quite different. His taste in music is
his mother's—the classics."

"His father was a jazz man, I take it?" I hinted.

"He preferred playing piano in dives, and breathing
smoke and drinking gin, to his wife and child and home
and job. Herbert's mother finally said he had to choose
one life or the other."

I nodded sympathetically. Maybe Herbert looked on
his fortune as filthy, untouchable, since it came from
his father's side of the family. "This grandfather of Herbert's, who died two years ago—?"

"He supported Herbert and his mother after his son
deserted them. Herbert worshipped him." She shook her
head sadly. "He was penniless when he died."

"What a shame."

"I'd so hoped he would leave us a little something, so
Herbert wouldn't have to work week ends."

WE WERE trying to talk above the clatter, tinkle and crash
of the cafeteria where Herbert ate every day. Lunch was
on me—or on my expense account—and I'd picked up
his check for eighty-seven cents. I said, "Now, Herbert,
before we go any further, we'd better decide what you
want from your investments: growth or income." It was
a cliché of the counseling business. God knows what
he wanted from the securities. It didn't seem to be what
everybody else wanted—money.

"Whatever you say," Herbert said absently. He was

upset about something, and not paying much attention to me.

"Herbert—look, you've got to face this thing. You're a rich man. You've got to concentrate on making the most of your holdings."

"That's why I called you. I want *you* to concentrate. I want you to run things for me, so I won't have to bother with the deposits and proxies and taxes. Don't trouble me with it at all."

"Your lawyers have been banking the dividends, eh?"

"Most of them. Took out thirty-two dollars for Christmas, and gave a hundred to the church."

"So what's your balance?"

He handed me the deposit book.

"Not bad," I said. Despite his Christmas splurge and largess toward the church, he'd managed to salt away $50,227.33. "May I ask what a man with a balance like that can be blue about?"

"Got bawled out at work again."

"Buy the place and burn it down," I suggested.

"I could, couldn't I?" A wild look came into his eyes, then disappeared.

"Herbert, you can do anything your heart desires."

"Oh, I suppose so. It's all in the way you look at it."

I leaned forward. "How *do* you look at it, Herbert?"

"I think every man, for his own self-respect, should earn what he lives on."

"But, Herbert—"

"I have a wonderful wife and child, a nice house for them, and a car. And I've earned every penny of the way. I'm living up to the full measure of my responsibilities. I'm proud to say I'm everything my mother wanted me to be, and nothing my father was."

"Do you mind my asking what your father was?"

"I don't enjoy talking about him. Home and family meant nothing to him. His real love was for low-down music and honky-tonks, and for the trash in them."

"Was he a good musician, do you think?"

"Good?" For an instant, there was excitement in his voice, and he tensed, as though he were going to make an important point. But he relaxed again. "Good?" he repeated, flatly this time. "Yes, in a crude way, I suppose he was passable—technically, that is."

"And that much you inherited from him."

"His wrists and hands, maybe. God help me if there's any more of him in me."

"You've got his love of music, too."

"I love music, but I'd never let it get like dope to me!" he said, with more force than seemed necessary.

"Uh-huh. Well—"

"Never!"

"Beg your pardon?"

His eyes were wide. "I said I'll never let music get like dope to me. It's important to me, but I'm master of it, and not the other way around."

APPARENTLY it was a treacherous subject, so I switched back to the matter of his finances. "Yes, well, now about your portfolio again: just what use do you expect to make of it?"

"Use some of it for Alma's and my old age; leave most of it to the boy."

"The least you can do is take enough out of the kitty to let you out of working week ends."

He stood up suddenly. "Look. I want you to handle my securities, not my life. If you can't do one without the other, I'll find someone who can."

"Please, Herbert, Mr. Foster. I'm sorry, sir. I was only trying to get the whole picture for planning."

He sat down, red-faced. "All right then, respect my convictions. I want to make my own way. If I have to hold a second job to make ends meet, then that's my cross to bear."

"Sure, sure, certainly. And you're dead right, Herbert. I respect you for it." I thought he belonged in the bughouse for it. "You leave everything to me from now on. I'll invest those dividends and run the whole show." As I puzzled over Herbert, I glanced at a passing blonde. Herbert said something I missed. "What was that, Herbert?"

"I said, 'If thy right eye offend thee, pluck it out and cast it from thee.' "

I laughed appreciatively, then cut it short. Herbert was deadly serious. "Well, pretty soon you'll have the car paid for, and then you can take a well-earned rest on the week ends. And you'll really have something to be proud of, eh? Earned the whole car by the sweat of your brow, right down to the tip of the exhaust pipe."

"One more payment."

"*Then* by-by, restaurant."

"There'll still be Alma's birthday present to pay for. I'm getting her television."

"Going to earn that, too, are you?"

"Think how much more meaningful it will be as a gift, if I do."

"Yes, sir, and it'll give her something to do on week ends, too."

"If I have to work week ends for twenty-eight more months, God knows it's little enough to do for her."

If the stock market kept doing what it had been doing for the past three years, Herbert would be a millionaire just about the time he made the last payment on Alma's birthday present. "Fine."

"I love my family," Herbert said earnestly.

"I'm sure you do."

"And I wouldn't trade the life I've got for anything."

"I can certainly see why," I said. I had the impression that he was arguing with me, that it was important to him that I be convinced.

"When I consider what my father was, and then see the life I've made for myself, it's the biggest thrill in all my experience."

A very small thrill could qualify for the biggest in Herbert's experience, I thought. "I envy you. It must be gratifying."

"Gratifying," he repeated determinedly. "It is, it is, it is."

MY FIRM began managing Herbert's portfolio, converting some of the slower-moving securities into more lucrative ones, investing the accumulated dividends, diversifying his holdings so he'd be in better shape to weather economic shifts—and in general making his fortune altogether ship-shape. A sound portfolio is a thing of beauty in its way, aside from its cash value. Putting one together is a creative act, if done right, with solid major themes of industrials, rails and utilities, and with the lighter, more exciting themes of electronics, frozen foods, magic drugs, oil and gas, aviation and other more speculative items. Herbert's portfolio was our masterpiece. I was thrilled and proud of what the firm had done, and not being able to show it off, even to him, was depressing.

It was too much for me, and I decided to engineer a coincidence. I would find out in which restaurant Herbert worked, and then drop in, like any other citizen, for something to eat. I would happen to have a report on his overhauled portfolio with me.

I telephoned Alma, who told me the name of the place, one I'd never heard of. Herbert hadn't wanted to talk about the place, so I gathered that it was pretty grim —as he said, his cross to bear.

It was worse than I'd expected: tough, brassy, dark and noisy. Herbert had picked one hell of a place, indeed, to do penance for a wayward father, or to demonstrate his gratitude to his wife, or to maintain his self-respect by earning his own way—or to do whatever it was he was doing there.

I elbowed my way between bored-looking women and race-track types to the bar. I had to shout at the bartender to be heard. When I did get through to him, he yelled back that he'd never heard of no Herbert Foster. Herbert, then, was about as minor an employee as there was in the establishment. He was probably doing something greasy in the kitchen or basement. Typical.

In the kitchen, a crone was making questionable-looking hamburgers, and nipping at a quart of beer.

"I'm looking for Herbert Foster."

"Ain' no damn' Herbert Foster in here."

"In the basement?"

"Ain' no damn' basement."

"Ever hear of Herbert Foster?"

"Ain't never heard of no damn' Herbert Foster."

"Thanks."

I sat in a booth to think it over. Herbert had apparently picked the joint out of a telephone book, and told Alma it was where he spent his week-end evenings. In a way, it made me feel better, because it began to look as though Herbert maybe had better reasons than he'd given me for letting eight hundred and fifty thousand dollars get musty. I remembered that every time I'd mentioned his giving up the week-end job, he'd reacted like a man hearing a dentist tune up his drill. I saw it now: the minute he let Alma know he was rich, he'd lose his excuse for getting away from her on week ends.

But what was it that was worth more to Herbert than

eight hundred and fifty thousand? Binges? Dope? Women? I sighed, and admitted I was kidding myself, that I was no closer to the answer than I'd ever been. Moral turpitude on Herbert's part was inconceivable. Whatever he was up to, it had to be for a good cause. His mother had done such a thorough job on him, and he was so awfully ashamed of his father's failings, that I was sure he couldn't operate any other way but righteously. I gave up on the puzzle, and ordered a nightcap.

And then Herbert Foster, looking drab and hunted, picked his way through the crowd. His expression was one of disapproval, of a holy man in Babylon. He was oddly stiff-necked and held his arms at his sides as he pointedly kept from brushing against anyone or from meeting any of the gazes that fell upon him. There was no question that being in the place was absolute, humiliating hell for him.

I called to him, but he paid no attention. There was no communicating with him. Herbert was in a near coma of see-no-evil, speak-no-evil, hear-no-evil.

The crowd in the rear parted for him, and I expected to see Herbert go into a dark corner for a broom or a mop. But a light flashed on at the far end of the aisle the crowd made for him, and a tiny white piano sparkled there like jewelry. The bartender set a drink on the piano, and went back to his post.

Herbert dusted off the piano bench with his handkerchief, and sat down gingerly. He took a cigarette from his breast pocket and lighted it. And then the cigarette started to droop slowly from his lips; and, as it drooped, Herbert hunched over the keyboard and his eyes narrowed as though he were focusing on something beautiful on a faraway horizon.

Startlingly, Herbert Foster disappeared. In his place sat an excited stranger, his hands poised like claws. Suddenly he struck, and a spasm of dirty, low-down, gorgeous jazz shook the air, a hot wraith of the twenties.

LATE that night I went over my masterpiece, the portfolio of Herbert Foster, alias "Firehouse" Harris. I hadn't bothered Firehouse with it or with myself.

In a week or so, there would be a juicy melon from one of his steel companies. Three of his oil stocks were paying extra dividends. The farm machinery company in which he owned five thousand shares was about to offer him rights worth three dollars apiece.

Thanks to me and my company and an economy in full bloom, Herbert was about to be several thousand dollars richer than he'd been a month before. I had a right to be proud, but my triumph—except for the commission—was gall and wormwood.

Nobody could do anything for Herbert. Herbert already had what he wanted. He had had it long before the inheritance or I intruded. He had the respectability his mother had hammered into him. But just as priceless as that was an income not quite big enough to go around. It left him no alternative but—in the holy names of wife, child and home—to play piano in a dive, and breathe smoke and drink gin, to be Firehouse Harris, his father's son, three nights out of seven.

Deer in
the Works

THE big black stacks of the Ilium Works of the Federal Apparatus Corporation spewed acid fumes and soot over the hundreds of men and women who were lined up before the red-brick employment office. The Ilium Works, already the second-largest industrial plant in America, was increasing its staff by one third in order to meet armament contracts. Every ten minutes or so, a company policeman opened the employment-office door, letting out a chilly gust from the air-conditioned interior and admitting three more applicants.

"Next three," said the policeman sleepily.

A middle-sized man in his late twenties, his young face camouflaged with a mustache and spectacles, was admitted after a four-hour wait. His spirits and the new suit he'd bought for the occasion were wilted by the fumes and the August sun, and he'd given up lunch in order to keep his place in line. But his bearing remained jaunty. He was the last, in his group of three, to face the receptionist.

"Screw-machine operator, ma'am," said the first man.

"See Mr. Cormody in booth seven," said the receptionist.

"Plastic extrusion, miss," said the next man.

"See Mr. Hoyt in booth two," she said. "Skill?" she asked the urbane young man in the wilted suit. "Milling machine? Jig borer?"

"Writing," he said. "Any kind of writing."

"You mean advertising and sales promotion?"

"Yes—that's what I mean."

She looked doubtful. "Well, I don't know. We didn't put out a call for that sort of people. You can't run a machine, can you?"

"Typewriter," he said jokingly.

The receptionist was a sober young woman. "The company does not use male stenographers," she said. "See Mr. Dilling in booth twenty-six. He just might know of some advertising-and-sales-promotion-type job."

He straightened his tie and coat, forced a smile that implied he was looking into jobs at the Works as sort of a lark. He walked into booth twenty-six and extended his hand to Mr. Dilling, a man of his own age. "Mr. Dilling, my name is David Potter. I was curious to know what openings you might have in advertising and sales promotion, and thought I'd drop in for a talk."

Mr. Dilling, an old hand at facing young men who tried to hide their eagerness for a job, was polite but outwardly unimpressed. "Well, you came at a bad time, I'm afraid, Mr. Potter. The competition for that kind of job is pretty stiff, as you perhaps know, and there isn't much of anything open just now."

David nodded. "I see." He had had no experience in asking for a job with a big organization, and Mr. Dilling was making him aware of what a fine art it was—if you couldn't run a machine. A duel was under way.

"But have a seat anyway, Mr. Potter."

"Thank you." He looked at his watch. "I really ought to be getting back to my paper soon."

"You work on a paper around here?"

"Yes. I own a weekly paper in Dorset, about ten miles from Ilium."

"Oh—you don't say. Lovely little village. Thinking of giving up the paper, are you?"

"Well, no—not exactly. It's a possibility. I bought the

paper soon after the war, so I've been with it for eight years, and I don't want to go stale. I might be wise to move on. It all depends on what opens up."

"You have a family?" said Mr. Dilling pleasantly.

"Yes. My wife, and two boys and two girls."

"A nice, big, well-balanced family," said Mr. Dilling. "And you're so young, too."

"Twenty-nine," said David. He smiled. "We didn't plan it to be quite that big. It's run to twins. The boys are twins, and then, several days ago, the girls came."

"You don't say!" said Mr. Dilling. He winked. "That would certainly start a young man thinking about getting a little security, eh, with a family like that?"

Both of them treated the remark casually, as though it were no more than a pleasantry between two family men. "It's what we wanted, actually, two boys, two girls," said David. "We didn't expect to get them this quickly, but we're glad now. As far as security goes—well, maybe I flatter myself, but I think the adminstrative and writing experience I've had running the paper would be worth a good bit to the right people, if something happened to the paper."

"One of the big shortages in this country," said Dilling philosophically, concentrating on lighting a cigarette, "is men who know how to do things, and know how to take responsibility and get things done. I only wish there were better openings in advertising and sales promotion than the ones we've got. They're important, interesting jobs, understand, but I don't know how you'd feel about the starting salary."

"Well, I'm just trying to get the lay of the land, now —to see how things are. I have no idea what salary industry might pay a man like me, with my experience."

"The question experienced men like yourself usually ask is: how high can I go and how fast? And the answer to that is that the sky is the limit for a man with drive and creative ambition. And he can go up fast or slow, depending on what he's willing to do and capable of putting into the job. We might start out a man like you at, oh, say, a hundred dollars a week, but that isn't to say you'd be stuck at that level for two years or even two months."

"I suppose a man could keep a family on that until he got rolling," said David.

"You'd find the work in the publicity end just about the same as what you're doing now. Our publicity people have high standards for writing and editing and reporting, and our publicity releases don't wind up in newspaper editors' wastebaskets. Our people do a professional job, and are well-respected as journalists." He stood. "I've got a little matter to attend to—take me about ten minutes. Could you possibly stick around? I'm enjoying our talk."

David looked at his watch. "Oh—guess I could spare another ten or fifteen minutes."

Dilling was back in his booth in three minutes, chuckling over some private joke. "Just talking on the phone with Lou Flammer, the publicity supervisor. Needs a new stenographer. Lou's a card. Everybody here is crazy about Lou. Old weekly man himself, and I guess that's where he learned to be so easy to get along with. Just to feel him out for the hell of it, I told him about you. I didn't commit you to anything—just said what you told me, that you were keeping your eyes open. And guess what Lou said?"

"Guess what, Nan," said David Potter to his wife on the telephone. He was wearing only his shorts, and was phoning from the company hospital. "When you come home from the hospital tomorrow, you'll be coming home to a solid citizen who pulls down a hundred and ten dollars a week, *every* week. I just got my badge and passed my physical!"

"Oh?" said Nan, startled. "It happened awfully fast, didn't it? I didn't think you were going to plunge right in."

"What's there to wait for?"

"Well—I don't know. I mean, how do you know what you're getting into? You've never worked for anybody but yourself, and don't know anything about getting along in a huge organization. I knew you were going to talk to the Ilium people about a job, but I thought you planned to stick with the paper another year, anyway."

"In another year I'll be thirty, Nan."

"Well?"

"That's pretty old to be starting a career in industry. There are guys my age here who've been working their way up for ten years. That's pretty stiff competition, and it'll be that much stiffer a year from now. And how do we know Jason will still want to buy the paper a year from now?" Ed Jason was David's assistant, a recent college graduate whose father wanted to buy the paper for him. "And this job that opened up today in publicity won't be open a year from now, Nan. Now was the time to switch—this afternoon!"

Nan sighed. "I suppose. But it doesn't seem like you. The Works are fine for some people; they seem to thrive on that life. But you've always been so free. And you love the paper—you know you do."

"I do," said David, "and it'll break my heart to let it go. It was a swell thing to do when we had no kids, but it's a shaky living now—with the kids to educate and all."

"But, hon," said Nan, "the paper is making money."

"It could fold like that," said David, snapping his fingers. "A daily could come in with a one-page insert of Dorset news, or—"

"Dorset likes its little paper too much to let that happen. They like you and the job you're doing too much."

David nodded. "What about ten years from now?"

"What about ten years from now in the Works? What about ten years from now anywhere?"

"It's a better bet that the Works will still be here. I haven't got the right to take long chances any more, Nan, not with a big family counting on me."

"It won't be a very happy big family, darling, if you're not doing what you want to do. I want you to go on being happy the way you have been—driving around the countryside, getting news and talking and selling ads; coming home and writing what you want to write, what you believe in. You in the Works!"

"It's what I've got to do."

"All right, if you say so. I've had my say."

"It's still journalism, high-grade journalism," said David.

"Just don't sell the paper to Jason right away. Put him in charge, but let's wait a month or so, please?"

"No sense in waiting, but if you really want to, all right." David held up a brochure he'd been handed after his physical examination was completed. "Listen to this, Nan: under the company Security Package, I get ten dollars a day for hospital expenses in case of illness, full pay for twenty-six weeks, a hundred dollars for special hospital expenses. I get life insurance for about half what it would cost on the outside. For whatever I put into government bonds under the payroll-savings plan, the company will give me a five per cent bonus in company stock—twelve years from now. I get two weeks' vacation with pay each year, and, after fifteen years, I get three weeks. Get free membership in the company country club. After twenty-five years, I'll be eligible for a pension of at least a hundred and twenty-five dollars a month, and much more if I rise in the organization and stick with it for more than twenty-five years!"

"Good heavens!" said Nan.

"I'd be a damn fool to pass that up, Nan."

"I still wish you'd waited until the little girls and I were home and settled, and you got used to them. I feel you were panicked into this."

"No, no—this is it, Nan. Give the little girls a kiss apiece for me. I've got to go now, and report to my new supervisor."

"Your what?"

"Supervisor."

"Oh. I thought that's what you said, but I couldn't be sure."

"Good-by, Nan."

"Good-by, David."

DAVID clipped his badge to his lapel, and stepped out of the hospital and onto the hot asphalt floor of the world within the fences of the Works. Dull thunder came from the buildings around him, a truck honked irritably at him, and a cinder blew in his eye. He dabbed at the cinder with a corner of his handkerchief and finally got it out. When his vision was restored, he looked about himself for Building 31, where his new office and supervisor were. Four busy streets fanned out from where he stood, and each stretched seemingly to infinity.

He stopped a passer-by who seemed in less of a desperate hurry than the rest. "Could you tell me, please, how to find Building 31, Mr. Flammer's office?"

The man he asked was old and bright-eyed, apparently getting as much pleasure from the clangor and smells and nervous activity of the Works as David would have gotten from April in Paris. He squinted at David's badge and then at his face. "Just starting out, are you?"

"Yes sir. My first day."

"What do you know about that?" The old man shook his head wonderingly, and winked. "Just starting out. Building 31? Well, sir, when I first came to work here in 1899, you could see Building 31 from here, with nothing between us and it but mud. Now it's all built up. See that water tank up there, about a quarter of a mile? Well, Avenue 17 branches off there, and you follow that almost to the end, then cut across the tracks, and— Just starting out, eh? Well, I'd better walk you up there. Came here for just a minute to talk to the pension folks, but that can wait. I'd enjoy the walk."

"Thank you."

"Fifty-year man, I was," he said proudly, and he led David up avenues and alleys, across tracks, over ramps and through tunnels, through buildings filled with spitting, whining, grumbling machinery, and down identical corridors with green walls and numbered black doors.

"Can't be a fifty-year man no more," said the old man pityingly. "Can't come to work until you're eighteen nowadays, and you got to retire when you're sixty-five." He poked his thumb under his lapel to make a small gold button protrude. On it was the number "50" superimposed on the company trade-mark. "Something none of you youngsters can look forward to wearing some day, no matter how much you want one."

"Very nice button," said David.

The old man pointed out a door. "Here's Flammer's office. Keep your mouth shut till you find out who's who and what *they* think. Good luck."

Lou Flammer's secretary was not at her desk, so David walked to the door of the inner office and knocked.

"Yes?" said a man's voice sweetly. "Please come in."

David opened the door. "Mr. Flammer?"

Lou Flammer was a short, fat man in his early thirties. He beamed at David. "What can I do to help you?"

"I'm David Potter, Mr. Flammer."

Flammer's Santa-Claus-like demeanor decayed. He leaned back, propped his feet on his desk top, and stuffed a cigar, which he'd concealed in his cupped hand, into his large mouth. "Hell—thought you were a scoutmaster." He looked at his desk clock, which was mounted in a miniature of the company's newest automatic dishwasher. "Boy scouts touring the Works. Supposed to stop in here fifteen minutes ago for me to give 'em a talk on scouting and industry. Fifty-six per cent of Federal Apparatus' executives were eagle scouts."

David started to laugh, but found himself doing it all alone, and he stopped. "Amazing figure," he said.

"It *is*," said Flammer judiciously. "Says something for scouting and something for industry. Now, before I tell you where your desk is, I'm supposed to explain the rating-sheet system. That's what the Manual says. Dilling tell you about that?"

"Not that I recall. There was an awful lot of information all at once."

"Well, there's nothing much to it," said Flammer. "Every six months a rating sheet is made out on you, to let you and to let us know just where you stand, and what sort of progress you've been making. Three people who've been close to your work make out independent ratings of you, and then all the information is brought together on a master copy—with carbons for you, me, and Personnel, and the original for the head of the Advertising and Sales Promotion Division. It's very helpful for everybody, you most of all, if you take it the right way." He waved a rating sheet before David. "See? Blanks for appearance, loyalty, promptness, initiative, co-operativeness—things like that. You'll make out rating sheets on other people, too, and whoever does the rating is anonymous."

"I see." David felt himself reddening with resentment. He fought the emotion, telling himself his reaction was a small-town man's—and that it would do him good to learn to think as a member of a great, efficient team.

"Now about pay, Potter," said Flammer, "there'll never be any point in coming in to ask me for a raise. That's all done on the basis of the rating sheets and the salary curve." He rummaged through his drawers and found a graph, which he spread out on his desk. "Here—now you see this curve? Well, it's the average salary curve for men with college educations in the company. See—you can follow it on up. At thirty, the average man makes this much; at forty, this much—and so on. Now, this curve above it shows what men with real growth potential can make. See? It's a little higher and curves upward a little faster. You're how old?"

"Twenty-nine," said David, trying to see what the salary figures were that ran along one side of the graph.

Flammer saw him doing it, and pointedly kept them hidden with his forearm.

"Uh-huh." Flammer wet the tip of a pencil with his tongue, and drew a small "x" on the graph, squarely astride the average man's curve. "There *you* are!"

David looked at the mark, and then followed the curve with his eyes across the paper, over little bumps, up gentle slopes, along desolate plateaus, until it died abruptly at the margin which represented age sixty-five. The graph left no questions to be asked and was deaf to argument. David looked from it to the human being he would also be dealing with. "You had a weekly once, did you, Mr. Flammer?"

Flammer laughed. "In my naïve, idealistic youth, Potter, I sold ads to feed stores, gathered gossip, set type, and wrote editorials that were going to save the world, by God."

David smiled admiringly. "What a circus, eh?"

"Circus?" said Flammer. "Freak show, maybe. It's a good way to grow up fast. Took me about six months to find out I was killing myself for peanuts, that a little guy couldn't even save a village three blocks long, and that the world wasn't worth saving anyway. So I started looking out for Number One. Sold out to a chain, came down here, and here I am."

The telephone rang. "Yes?" said Flammer sweetly. "Puh-*bliss*-itee." His benign smile faded. "No. You're kidding, aren't you? Where? Really—this is no gag? All right, all right. Lord! What a time for this to happen. I haven't got anybody here, and I can't get away on account of the goddam boy scouts." He hung up. "Potter—you've got your first assignment. There's a deer loose in the Works!"

"Deer?"

"Don't know how he got in, but he's in. Plumber went to fix a drinking fountain out at the softball diamond across from Building 217, and flushed a deer out from under the bleachers. Now they got him cornered up around the metallurgy lab." He stood and hammered on his desk. "Murder! The story will go all over the country, Potter. Talk about human interest. Front page! Of all the times for Al Tappin to be out at the Ashtabula Works taking pictures of a new viscometer they cooked up out there! All right—I'll call up a hack photographer downtown, Potter, and get him to meet you out by the metallurgy lab. You get the story and see that he gets the right shots. Okay?"

He led David into the hallway. "Just go back the way you came, turn left instead of right at fractional horsepower motors, cut through hydraulic engineering, catch bus eleven on Avenue 9, and it'll take you right there. After you get the story and pictures, we'll get them cleared by the law division, the plant security officer, our department head and buildings and grounds, and shoot them right out. Now get going. That deer isn't on the payroll—he isn't going to wait for you. Come to work today—tomorrow your work will be on every front page in the country, if we can get it approved. The name of the photographer you're going to meet is McGarvey. Got it? You're in the big time now, Potter. We'll all be watching." He shut the door behind David.

David found himself trotting down the hall, down a stairway, and into an alley, brushing roughly past persons in a race against time. Many turned to watch the purposeful young man with admiration.

On and on he strode, his mind seething with information: *Flammer, Building 31; deer, metallurgy lab; photographer, Al Tappin. No. Al Tappin in Ashtabula.* Flenny *the hack photographer. No.* McCammer. *No.* McCammer is new supervisor. Fifty-six per cent eagle scouts. Deer by viscometer laboratory. No. Viscometer in Ashtabula. Call Danner, new supervisor, and get instructions right. Three weeks' vacation after fifteen years. Danner not new supervisor. Anyway, new supervisor in Building 319. No. Fanner in Building 39981983319.

David stopped, blocked by a grimy window at the end of a blind alley. All he knew was that he'd never been there before, that his memory had blown a gasket, and that the deer was not on the payroll. The air in the alley was thick with tango music and the stench of scorched insulation. David scrubbed away some of the crust on the window with his handkerchief, praying for a glimpse of something that made sense.

Inside were ranks of women at benches, rocking their heads in time to the music, and dipping soldering irons into great nests of colored wires that crept past them on endless belts. One of them looked up and saw David, and winked in tango rhythm. David fled.

At the mouth of the alley, he stopped a man and asked him if he'd heard anything about a deer in the Works. The man shook his head and looked at David oddly, making David aware of how frantic he must look. "I heard it was out by the lab," David said more calmly.

"Which lab?" said the man.

"That's what I'm not sure of," said David. "There's more than one?"

"Chemical lab?" said the man. "Materials testing lab? Paint lab? Insulation lab?"

"No—I don't think it's any of those," said David.

"Well, I could stand here all afternoon naming labs, and probably not hit the right one. Sorry, I've got to go. You don't know what building they've got the differential analyzer in, do you?"

"Sorry," said David. He stopped several other people, none of whom knew anything about the deer, and he tried to retrace his steps to the office of his supervisor, whatever his name was. He was swept this way and that by the currents of the Works, stranded in backwaters, sucked back into the main stream, and his mind was more and more numbed, and the mere reflexes of self-preservation were more and more in charge.

He chose a building at random, and walked inside for a momentary respite from the summer heat, and was deafened by the clangor of steel sheets being cut and punched, being smashed into strange shapes by great hammers that dropped out of the smoke and dust overhead. A hairy, heavily muscled man was seated near the door on a wooden stool, watching a giant lathe turn a bar of steel the size of a small silo.

David now had the idea of going through a company phone directory until he recognized his supervisor's name. He called to the machinist from a few feet away, but his voice was lost in the din. He tapped the man's shoulder. "Telephone around here?"

The man nodded. He cupped his hands around David's ear, and shouted. "Up that, and through the——" Down crashed a hammer. "Turn left and keep going until you——" An overhead crane dropped a stack of steel plates. "Four doors down from there is it. Can't miss it."

David, his ears ringing and his head aching, walked into the street again and chose another door. Here was peace and air conditioning. He was in the lobby of an auditorium, where a group of men were examining a box studded with dials and switches that was spotlighted and mounted on a revolving platform.

"Please, miss," he said to a receptionist by the door, "could you tell me where I could find a telephone?"

"It's right around the corner, sir," she said. "But I'm afraid no one is permitted here today but the crystallographers. Are you with them?"

"Yes," said David.

"Oh—well, come right in. Name?"

He told her, and a man sitting next to her lettered it on a badge the size of a piepan. The badge was hung on his chest, and David headed for the telephone. A grinning, bald, big-toothed man, wearing a badge that said, "Stan Dunkel, Sales," caught him and steered him to the display.

"Dr. Potter," said Dunkel, "I ask you: is that the way to build an X-ray spectrogoniometer, or is that the way to build an X-ray spectrogoniometer?"

"Yes," said David. "That's the way, all right."

"Martini, Dr. Potter?" said a maid, offering a tray.

David emptied a Martini in one gloriously hot, stinging gulp.

"What features do you want in an X-ray Spectrogoniometer, Doctor?" said Dunkel.

"It should be sturdy, Mr. Dunkel," said David, and he left Dunkel there, pledging his reputation that there wasn't a sturdier one on earth.

In the phone booth, David had barely got through the telephone directory's A's before the name of his supervisor miraculously returned to his consciousness: *Flammer*! He found the number and dialed.

"Mr. Flammer's office," said a woman.

"Could I speak to him, please? This is David Potter."

"Oh—Mr. Potter. Well, Mr. Flammer is somewhere out in the Works now, but he left a message for you. He said there's an added twist on the deer story. When they catch the deer, the venison is going to be used at the Quarter-Century Club picnic."

"Quarter-Century Club?" said David.

"Oh, that's really something, Mr. Potter. It's for people who've been with the company twenty-five years or more. Free drinks and cigars, and just the best of everything. They have a wonderful time."

"Anything else about the deer?"

"Nothing he hasn't already told you," she said, and she hung up.

David Potter, with a third Martini in his otherwise empty stomach, stood in front of the auditorium and looked both ways for a deer.

"But our X-ray spectrogoniometer *is* sturdy, Dr. Potter," Stan Dunkel called to him from the auditorium steps.

Across the street was a patch of green, bordered by hedges. David pushed through the hedges into the outfield of a softball diamond. He crossed it and went behind the bleachers, where there was cool shade, and he sat down with his back to a wire-mesh fence which separated one end of the Works from a deep pine woods. There were two gates in the fence, but both were wired shut.

David was going to sit there for just a moment, long enough to get his nerve back, to take bearings. Maybe he could leave a message for Flammer, saying he'd suddenly fallen ill, which was essentially true, or—

"There he goes!" cried somebody from the other side of the diamond. There were gleeful cries, shouted orders, the sounds of men running.

A deer with broken antlers dashed under the bleachers, saw David, and ran frantically into the open again along the fence. He ran with a limp, and his reddish-brown coat was streaked with soot and grease.

"Easy now! Don't rush him! Just keep him there. Shoot into the woods, not the Works."

David came out from under the bleachers to see a great semicircle of men, several ranks deep, closing in slowly on the corner of fence in which the deer was at bay. In the front rank were a dozen company policemen with drawn pistols. Other members of the posse carried sticks and rocks and lariats hastily fashioned from wire.

The deer pawed the grass, and bucked and jerked its broken antlers in the direction of the crowd.

"Hold it!" shouted a familiar voice. A company limousine rumbled across the diamond to the back of the crowd. Leaning out of a window was Lou Flammer, David's supervisor. "Don't shoot until we get a picture of him alive," commanded Flammer. He pulled a photographer out of the limousine, and pushed him into the front rank.

Flammer saw David standing alone by the fence, his back to a gate. "Good boy, Potter," called Flammer. "Right on the ball! Photographer got lost, and I had to bring him here myself."

The photographer fired his flash bulbs. The deer bucked and sprinted along the fence toward David. David unwired the gate, opened it wide. A second later the deer's white tail was flashing through the woods and gone.

The profound silence was broken first by the whistling of a switch engine and then by the click of a latch as David stepped into the woods and closed the gate behind him. He didn't look back.

Hal Irwin's
Magic Lamp

HAL IRWIN built his magic lamp in his basement in Indianapolis, in the summer of 1929. It was supposed to look like Aladdin's lamp. What it was was an old tin teapot with a piece of cotton stuck in the spout for a wick. Hal bored a hole in the side for a doorbell button which he hooked up to two flashlight batteries and a buzzer inside.

It was supposed to be a cute way to call servants. You'd rub the lamp as if it were a magic lamp, and you'd push the button on the side. The buzzer'd go off, and a servant, if you had one, would come and ask you what you wished.

Hal didn't have a servant, but he was going to get one —a servant, and a whole lot else besides. Hal was a customer's man in a brokerage house, and he knew his business inside out. He'd made half a million dollars on the stock market, and nobody knew it. Not even his wife.

He made the magic lamp as a surprise for his wife. He was going to tell her it was a magic lamp. And then he was going to rub it and wish for a big new house, a big new Marmon, a big new everything. And then he was going to prove to her that it really was a magic lamp, because every wish was going to come true.

When he made the lamp, the interior decorator was finishing up the insides of the big new French chateau Hal had ordered built out on North Meridian Street.

When Hal made that lamp, he and Mary were living in a shotgun house down in all the soot at Seventeenth and Illinois Street. They'd been married two years, and Hal hadn't had her out more than half a dozen times. He wasn't being stingy. He was just saving up to buy her all the happiness a girl could ever ask for, and he was going to hand it to her in one fell swoop.

Hal was ten years older than Mary, so it was easy for him to buffalo her about a lot of things, and one of the things was money. He wouldn't talk money with her, never let her see a bill or a bank statement, never told her how much he made or what he was doing with it. All Mary had to go by was the piddling little allowance he gave her to run the house, so she guessed they were poor.

Mary didn't mind that at all. That girl was as wholesome as a peach and a glass of milk. Being poor gave her room to swing her religion around. When the end of the month came, and they'd eaten pretty well, and she hadn't asked Hal for an extra dime, she felt like a little white lamb. And she thought Hal was happy, even though he was broke, because she was giving him a hundred million dollars' worth of love.

There was only one thing about being poor that really bothered Mary, and that was the way Hal always seemed to think she wanted to be rich. She did her best to convince him that wasn't true.

When Hal would carry on about how well other folks were doing—about all the high life at the country clubs and the lakes—Mary'd talk about the millions of folks in China who didn't have a roof over their heads, or anything to eat.

"Me doing velly well for Chinaman," Hal said one night.

"You're doing very well for an American or for an anything!" Mary said. She hugged him, so he'd be proud and strong and happy.

"Well, your successful Chinaman's got a piece of news

for you," Hal said. "Tomorrow you're gonna get a cook.
I told an employment agency to send one out.

Mary was a wonderful cook, so he'd really hit her
where she lived. "Honey—are the meals that bad?" she
said.

"They're great," Hal said. "I have no complaints whatsoever."

"Then why should we get a cook?"

He looked at her as though she must be deaf, dumb,
and blind. "Don't you ever think of my pride?" he asked.

"Honey-bunch," he said, "don't tell me again about
people dying like flies in China. I am who I am where
I am, and I've got pride."

Mary looked down and wanted to cry. Here she
thought she'd been making Hal feel better all the time, and
she'd been making him feel worse instead.

"What do you think I think every time I see Bea
Muller or Nancy Gossett, downtown in their fur coats,
buying out the department stores?" Hal said. "I think
about you, stuck in this house. I think, 'Well, for crying
out loud, I used to be president of their husbands' fra-
ternity house!' For crying out loud, me and Harve Muller and George Gossett used to be the Grand Triumvirate in college. That's what they used to call us—the
Grand Triumvirate! We used to run the college, and I'm
not kidding. We founded Owl and Hammer!

"Look where they live and look where we live," Hal
went on. "We oughta be right out there with 'em at Fifty-
seventh and North Meridian! We oughta have a cottage
right next to 'em up at Lake Maxinkuckee! Least I can
do is get my wife a cook," Hal said.

So that was that. The next day the employment
agency sent out a colored woman named Ella Washington.

ELLA WASHINGTON was as bad off as anybody in China.
She was hungry and scared, and all alone in the world.
She was pregnant, and her husband had ditched her after
taking the four dollars from the sugar bowl. She was
wearing a pair of golden evening slippers some kind soul
had given her, and the heels were worn down to a nub.

"Folks at the agency said you'd be willin' to try me fo'
a week," Ella said to Mary. There wasn't any hope in the
way she said it. She didn't figure on lasting more'n that
one week. She was no older than Mary, but she'd been

kicked from pillar to post so much she'd come all unstuffed.

Mary got a lump in her throat, and she knew she could never send this poor soul away. "Come on in," she said.

Ella's tired feet capsized in those evening slippers, and it was all she could do to straighten them up again. "One thing I gotta tell you," she said. "I'm goan have a baby."

"I'll show you to your room," Mary said.

It turned out Ella couldn't cook worth a nickel. And she was so pooped out from being lonely and being poor and carrying the baby, she wasn't any great shakes at cleaning, either. So Mary had to work about three times as hard as she had before she got help.

"Ella," Mary said to her the first evening, while they were getting supper, "my husband keeps thinking I ought to want more than I've got. But you want to know something, Ella?"

"Yes'm," Ella said.

"You've got the only thing I really want," Mary said.

Ella looked at Mary as if Mary was crazy. "I do?" she said.

"A baby," Mary said. "Apparently the good Lord has seen fit not to give us one."

"Sometimes," Ella said, "I think the good Lawd oughta come down fo' jus' one day, an' fix things so's folks can swap aroun'." Her feet capsized again.

"That's what they sent?" Hal said, when he got home from work and took a look at the new cook.

"She's very good," Mary said.

"She's gonna have a baby," Hal said.

"Lots of people have babies," Mary said.

After supper, Hal went out in the kitchen and had a long talk with Ella. He told her what she was supposed to do the next Sunday. They were going out to a big new house, and Ella was supposed to go hide in the kitchen broom closet there, and put on a turban she'd find hanging inside.

When she heard a buzzer, she was supposed to come out and tell Mary the house was hers.

"What kine buzzer this goan be?" Ella asked him.

Hal went down in the basement and brought up the lamp and buzzed the buzzer once. Then he ran downstairs and hid it again behind the furnace.

Next Sunday, after dinner, Hall said why didn't they take Ella out for some fresh air in the automobile? That sounded like a nice idea, so they went riding out North Meridian Street, looking at all the big houses going up. Every time Hal would point out one he thought was pretty good, Mary would say she didn't want it. After a while Hal turned into the driveway of a brand-new French chateau. It was right between Harve Muller's Tudor manor and George Gossett's Spanish Mission. It was grander than either one.

"Why are we stopping here?" Mary asked.

"House of a friend of mine," Hal said. "I've got a package for him." He got the package out of the trunk, and told Mary and Ella to come on in and see the house.

"What's in the package?" Mary said.

"Aladdin's lamp, honey," Hal said. He opened the package and showed the lamp to Mary. "That's how my friend got this house," he said. "He just rubbed this lamp and wished for it."

"Go on," Mary said.

Hal pushed open the front door without knocking, and walked right in. "Ella," he said, "why don't you go out in the kitchen and see what a real kitchen looks like."

They went out in the kitchen a minute later and there wasn't any sign of Ella. Hal hollered for her, and finally he said there wasn't but one thing to do, and that was to rub the lamp and tell the jinni to go find her.

"Oh, heck," Hal said, "as long as we're gonna get the jinni here anyway, why don't we ask it for the house, too?" He closed his eyes. "Oh, spirit of the sky and under the earth and in the sea," he said, "appear, jinni, and grant that my wife can have this house!" He pushed the doorbell button on the side of the lamp, and the buzzer went off.

The door of the broom closet flew open. Out came Ella. On her head was a turban Hal had made out of a bath towel. He'd pinned a big fake ruby to its front.

"OH, welcome home, mistress!" Ella said to Mary. "This home is yo's! Yo' husband's rich! Yo' slightest wish is my command!"

"Jinni!" Hal said.

"Yessuh?" Ella said.

"Put a blue Marmon in the garage," Hal said. *Buzz* went the buzzer.

"It's there," Ella said.

"Jinni!" Hal said.

"Yessuh?" Ella said.

"Have movers go to our old house and bring our stuff up here," Hal said. *Buzz* went the buzzer.

"They's doin' it," Ella said.

"Jinni—how's about a cottage on Lake Maxinkuckee?" Hal said. *Buzz* went the buzzer.

"You got it," Ella said.

"And a membership in the Hoosier Highlands Golf and Country Club," Hal said. *Buzz* went the buzzer.

"Take it away," Ella said. She was having a pretty good time, except she was starting to go in labor.

"Jinni," Hal said, "I wish my wife would smile and say something." *Buzz* went the buzzer.

"It's—it's very nice," Mary said. She did something with her face muscles, and she hoped it looked like a smile from the outside.

She touched Hal softly on the cheek and wandered out the back door, pretending she was guzzling happiness.

Mary walked until she came to a large pear tree.

She narrowed her mind down to where she didn't have to think about anything but one lonesome pear hanging down in front of her. She picked it and ate it. She never forgot how it tasted. It was a good little pear, firm and gritty. Tasted like rock candy and lemon juice.

Hal and Ella followed her after a while. Hal was still buzzing the buzzer, just wishing up a storm.

"Jinni," Hal said, "this looks like a pretty good place for refreshments. I wish for a pitcher of something nice and cold in the icebox." *Buzz* went the buzzer.

"Yessuh," Ella said. Only she didn't move. She just stood there, rolling her eyes. "All this excitement, Mistuh Irwin—" Ella said. She was trying to apologize for something.

"What about it?" Hal said.

"I'm sorry, Mistuh Irwin," Ella said, "but I think the jinni's havin' a baby."

Mary still had the core of that good little pear in her hand when she got in the back seat of the new Marmon with Ella. Hal still had his magic lamp when he got in front and headed for the hospital.

"Oh, I sporled the day," Ella said. "Jinni went an' sporled the day."

"Don't you worry about it, Ella," Mary said. "Your baby is more important than any house."

"Sho' *feels* impawtent," Ella said. The pain passed. "There was s'posed to be a whole lot mo' wishin'," she said.

"All the wishes are for you and your baby right now," Mary said.

Hal didn't say anything. He blew his horn and ran through a red light.

"You happen to know what we're worth right now?" he said finally. He couldn't have put the question worse.

"What are we worth?" Mary said.

"Half a million," Hal said. "You can make a lot of wishes, and never make a dent in that."

"Hal," Mary said, "give me the lamp."

"What for?" Hal said.

"I want to make a wish," Mary said.

Hal handed the lamp back to her.

MARY rubbed the lamp and said, "I wish five thousand dollars for a college education for Ella's baby."

"Whaaaaaat?" Hal said.

Ella opened her eyes wide, and Mary looked in those eyes and saw back through ten million years of hopes and dreams.

"I'm goan name that baby after you, Miz Irwin, if it's a girl. I'm goan name it after Mistuh Irwin if it's a boy," Ella said.

"If it's a boy, name it Grand Triumvirate," Hal said.

"Yessuh," Ella said. "I do that." Then she groaned, and the biggest pain of all hit her. She hung on to the lamp with both hands, and squeezed.

Hall pulled up to the emergency door of the hospital, and Grand Triumvirate Washington was born right there, with the buzzer in Hal Irwin's magic lamp buzzing to beat the band.

The sun was going down when Hal and Mary came out of the hospital.

They got into their new Marmon.

Mary found the core of that good pear on the ground right outside her door. She picked it up and held it like it was a very valuable thing.

Hal fiddled with the lamp. Ella had squeezed it so hard

the lid wouldn't close any more. Hal pushed the button, and all that happened was a feeble little beep. The batteries were all worn out.

WHEN they got home to the new chateau, Mary got out of the car and disappeared. Hal finally found her sitting in a flower bed. There was a hump of dirt in front of her, and she was patting it down. She'd planted the pear core, just for something to do.

He sat down beside her. "You want to make a wish?" he said.

Beep went the buzzer.

"All I'm wishing now is that there'll be a big pear tree here someday," Mary said.

"Then I wish it, too," Hal said. *Peep* went the buzzer. "Anything else?" Hal said.

Mary looked down at the hump of dirt, and she watered it with tears. She was crying because Hal had thought he could make her happy with a big greedy day.

But she wasn't crying so much about greediness as she was about how her husband didn't even know her after living with her for two years. The big booby'd spent so much time dreaming about the old days, he'd just let that magic lamp take her two years right away from her.

Hal had diddled himself out of the two years, too—and he knew it. Every time he'd wished, he'd felt a little of himself disappear. And he'd realized too late that he'd wished away the good man his wife thought she had. He'd wished his marriage all to smithereens.

More than that—he'd got his dreams out where he could see them, made them all come true. There they were, and there he was, sitting in their shadow.

He handed Mary the lamp, and was ready to cry himself. "Honey," he said "you do the wishing. Wish whatever we oughta wish to make things right again."

Mary didn't rub the lamp. She just held it. "I wish—" she said, "I wish the lamp would take back the house and car and everything else, if only it'll give me back the husband I thought I had."

She pushed the button. *Weep* went the buzzer.

And that was the last sound it had in it. When Mary pushed the button again nothing happened. Hal went around back and threw the magic lamp into a brand new ash can.

The pear core Mary planted is a big tree now.

Grand Triumvirate Washington is a big, handsome man now. He's a doctor.

His mother never changed his name, even though Hal begged her to. She couldn't be prouder of him. It's Grand Trumpet this and Grand Trumpet that, and Grand Trumpet can do no wrong.

The Grand Triumvirate the boy was named after never did get together again. The stock market crashed three days later, the very day Hal opened a five thousand dollar savings account in Grand Triumvirate Washington's name. Hal and Harve and George all lost their houses and everything else they had in the crash, and they just slunk off in different directions.

Hal and Mary live in a nice little ranch house out in Broad Ripple now. The other day Hal took Mary and their pretty nineteen-year-old daughter, Sue, out for some fresh air in the automobile. They went riding down North Meridian Street, looking at all the big old houses.

AND then Hal, all of a sudden, turned into the driveway of a French chateau. It was right between what used to be Harve Muller's Tudor manor and George Gossett's Spanish mission. There were "For Sale" signs in front of all three houses, and not a sign of life around. Nobody wants big houses like them any more.

Hal wanted to show Sue and Mary a big pear tree in the yard. There wasn't but one pear on the tree, and they picked it and took it home.

When they got home, Mary sliced up that lonesome little pear in slivers. She laid out the slivers on one of her best plates, a dark blue plate with a gold rim.

She took the plate out in the rose garden, where Hal was sunning himself. Sue had gone off somewhere with some friends. Mary and Hal took half an hour to eat that one pear. They'd take teeny-weeny little bites, then they'd chew and taste, chew and taste. Everything there was to think about that pear they thought. Everything there was for people to feel about one of God's pears they felt.

And everything there was for Hal to think about Mary he thought. And everything there was for Hal to feel about one of God's women he felt.

And he was awed. Every wish that nice girl had made on that fool lamp had come true.

Tom Edison's Shaggy Dog

Two old men sat on a park bench one morning in the sunshine of Tampa, Florida—one trying doggedly to read a book he was plainly enjoying while the other, Harold K. Bullard, told him the story of his life in the full, round, head tones of a public address system. At their feet lay Bullard's Labrador retriever, who further tormented the aged listener by probing his ankles with a large, wet nose.

Bullard, who had been, before he retired, successful in many fields, enjoyed reviewing his important past. But he faced the problem that complicates the lives of cannibals—namely: that a single victim cannot be used over and over. Anyone who had passed the time of day with him and his dog refused to share a bench with them again.

So Bullard and his dog set out through the park each day in quest of new faces. They had had good luck this morning, for they had found this stranger right away, clearly a new arrival in Florida, still buttoned up tight in heavy serge, stiff collar and necktie, and with nothing better to do than read.

"Yes," said Bullard, rounding out the first hour of his lecture, "made and lost five fortunes in my time."

"So you said," said the stranger, whose name Bullard had neglected to ask. "Easy, boy. No, no, no, boy," he said to the dog, who was growing more aggressive toward his ankles.

"Oh? Already told you that, did I?" said Bullard.

"Twice."

"Two in real estate, one in scrap iron, and one in oil and one in trucking."

"So you said."

"I did? Yes, guess I did. Two in real estate, one in scrap iron, one in oil and one in trucking. Wouldn't take back a day of it."

"No, I suppose not," said the stranger. "Pardon me, but do you suppose you could move your dog somewhere else? He keeps—"

"Him?" said Bullard, heartily. "Friendliest dog in the world. Don't need to be afraid of him."

"I'm not afraid of him. It's just that he drives me crazy, sniffing at my ankles."

"Plastic," said Bullard, chuckling.

"What?"

"Plastic. Must be something plastic on your garters. By golly, I'll bet it's those little buttons. Sure as we're sitting here, those buttons must be plastic. That dog is nuts about plastic. Don't know why that is, but he'll sniff it out and find it if there's a speck around. Must be a deficiency in his diet, though, by gosh, he eats better than I do. Once he chewed up a whole plastic humidor. Can you beat it? *That's* the business I'd go into now, by glory, if the pill rollers hadn't told me to let up, to give the old ticker a rest."

"You could tie the dog to that tree over there," said the stranger.

"I get so darn' sore at all the youngsters these days!" said Bullard. "All of 'em mooning around about no frontiers any more. There never have been so many frontiers as there are today. You know what Horace Greeley would say today?"

"His nose is wet," said the stranger, and he pulled his ankles away, but the dog humped forward in patient pursuit. "Stop it, boy!"

"His wet nose shows he's healthy," said Bullard. " 'Go

plastic, young man!' That's what Greeley'd say. 'Go atom, young man!' "

The dog had definitely located the plastic buttons on the stranger's garters and was cocking his head one way and another, thinking out ways of bringing his teeth to bear on those delicacies.

"Scat!" said the stranger.

" 'Go electronic, young man!' " said Bullard. "Don't talk to me about no opportunity any more. Opportunity's knocking down every door in the country, trying to get in. When I was young, a man had to go out and find opportunity and drag it home by the ears. Nowadays——"

"Sorry," said the stranger, evenly. He slammed his book shut, stood and jerked his ankle away from the dog. "I've got to be on my way. So good day, sir."

He stalked across the park, found another bench, sat down with a sigh and began to read. His respiration had just returned to normal, when he felt the wet sponge of the dog's nose on his ankles again.

"Oh—it's you!" said Bullard, sitting down beside him. "He was tracking you. He was on the scent of something, and I just let him have his head. What'd I tell you about plastic?" He looked about contentedly. "Don't blame you for moving on. It was stuffy back there. No shade to speak of and not a sign of a breeze."

"Would the dog go away if I bought him a humidor?" said the stranger.

"Pretty good joke, pretty good joke," said Bullard, amiably. Suddenly he clapped the stranger on his knee. "Sa-ay, you aren't in plastics, are you? Here I've been blowing off about plastics, and for all I know that's your line."

"My line?" said the stranger crisply, laying down his book. "Sorry—I've never had a line. I've been a drifter since the age of nine, since Edison set up his laboratory next to my home, and showed me the intelligence analyzer."

"Edison?" said Bullard. "Thomas Edison, the inventor?"

"If you want to call him that, go ahead," said the stranger.

"If I *want* to call him that?"—Bullard guffawed—"I

guess I just will! Father of the light bulb and I don't know what all."

"If you want to think he invented the light bulb, go ahead. No harm in it." The stranger resumed his reading.

"Say, what is this?" said Bullard, suspiciously. "You pulling my leg? What's this about an intelligence analyzer? I never heard of that."

"Of course you haven't," said the stranger. "Mr. Edison and I promised to keep it a secret. I've never told anyone. Mr. Edison broke his promise and told Henry Ford, but Ford made him promise not to tell anybody else—for the good of humanity."

Bullard was entranced. "Uh, this intelligence analyzer," he said, "it analyzed intelligence, did it?"

"It was an electric butter churn," said the stranger.

"Seriously now," Bullard coaxed.

"Maybe it *would* be better to talk it over with someone," said the stranger. "It's a terrible thing to keep bottled up inside me, year in and year out. But how can I be sure that it won't go any further?"

"My word as a gentleman," Bullard assured him.

"I don't suppose I could find a stronger guarantee than that, could I?" said the stranger, judiciously.

"There is no stronger guarantee," said Bullard, proudly. "Cross my heart and hope to die!"

"Very well." The stranger leaned back and closed his eyes, seeming to travel backward through time. He was silent for a full minute, during which Bullard watched with awe and respect.

"It was back in the fall of eighteen seventy-nine," said the stranger at last, softly. "Back in the village of Menlo Park, New Jersey. I was a boy of nine. A young man we all thought was a wizard had set up a laboratory next door to my home, and there were flashes and crashes inside, and all sorts of scary goings on. The neighborhood children were warned to keep away, not to make any noise that would bother the wizard.

"I didn't get to know Edison right off, but his dog Sparky and I got to be steady pals. A dog a whole lot like yours, Sparky was, and we used to wrestle all over the neighborhood. Yes, sir, your dog is the image of Sparky."

"Is that so?" said Bullard, flattered.

"Gospel," replied the stranger. "Well, one day Sparky

and I were wrestling around, and we wrestled right up to the door of Edison's laboratory. The next thing I knew, Sparky had pushed me in through the door, and bam! I was sitting on the laboratory floor, looking up at Mr. Edison himself."

"Bet he was sore," said Bullard, delighted.

"You can bet I was scared," said the stranger. "I thought I was face to face with Satan himself. Edison had wires hooked to his ears and running down to a little black box in his lap! I started to scoot, but he caught me by my collar and made me sit down.

" 'Boy,' said Edison, 'it's always darkest before the dawn. I want you to remember that.'

" 'Yes, sir,' I said.

" 'For over a year, my boy,' Edison said to me, 'I've been trying to find a filament that will last in an incandescent lamp. Hair, string, splinters—nothing works. So while I was trying to think of something else to try, I started tinkering with another idea of mine, just letting off steam. I put this together,' he said, showing me the little black box. 'I thought maybe intelligence was just a certain kind of electricity, so I made this intelligence analyzer here. It works! You're the first one to know about it, my boy. But I don't know why you shouldn't be. It will be your generation that will grow up in the glorious new era when people will be as easily graded as oranges.' "

"I don't believe it!" said Bullard.

"May I be struck by lightning this very instant!" said the stranger. "And it did work, too. Edison had tried out the analyzer on the men in his shop, without telling them what he was up to. The smarter a man was, by gosh, the farther the needle on the indicator in the little black box swung to the right. I let him try it on me, and the needle just lay where it was and trembled. But dumb as I was, then is when I made my one and only contribution to the world. As I say, I haven't lifted a finger since."

"Whadja do?" said Bullard, eagerly.

"I said, 'Mr. Edison, sir, let's try it on the dog.' And I wish you could have seen the show that dog put on when I said it! Old Sparky barked and howled and scratched to get out. When he saw we meant business, that he wasn't going to get out, he made a beeline right for the intelligence analyzer and knocked it out of Edison's hands. But we cornered him, and Edison held him down while

I touched the wires to his ears. And would you believe it, that needle sailed clear across the dial, way past a little red pencil mark on the dial face!"

"The dog busted it," said Bullard.

" 'Mr. Edison, sir,' I said, 'what's that red mark mean?'

" 'My boy,' said Edison, 'it means that the instrument is broken, because that red mark is me.' "

"I'll say it was broken," said Bullard.

THE stranger said gravely, "But it wasn't broken. No, sir. Edison checked the whole thing, and it was in apple-pie order. When Edison told me that, it was then that Sparky, crazy to get out, gave himself away."

"How?" said Bullard, suspiciously.

"We really had him locked in, see? There were three locks on the door—a hook and eye, a bolt, and a regular knob and latch. That dog stood up, unhooked the hook, pushed the bolt back and had the knob in his teeth when Edison stopped him."

"No!" said Bullard.

"Yes!" said the stranger, his eyes shining. "And then is when Edison showed me what a great scientist he was. He was willing to face the truth, no matter how unpleasant it might be.

" 'So!' said Edison to Sparky. 'Man's best friend, huh? Dumb animal, huh?'

"That Sparky was a caution. He pretended not to hear. He scratched himself and bit fleas and went around growling at ratholes—anything to get out of looking Edison in the eye.

" 'Pretty soft, isn't it, Sparky?' said Edison. 'Let somebody else worry about getting food, building shelters and keeping warm, while you sleep in front of a fire or go chasing after the girls or raise hell with the boys. No mortgages, no politics, no war, no work, no worry. Just wag the old tail or lick a hand, and you're all taken care of.'

" 'Mr. Edison,' I said, 'do you mean to tell me that dogs are smarter than people?'

" 'Smarter?' said Edison. 'I'll tell the world! And what have I been doing for the past year? Slaving to work out a light bulb so dogs can play at night!'

" 'Look, Mr. Edison,' said Sparky, 'why not—' "

"Hold on!" roared Bullard.

"Silence!" shouted the stranger, triumphantly. " 'Look, Mr. Edison,' said Sparky, 'why not keep quiet about this? It's been working out to everybody's satisfaction for hundreds of thousands of years. Let sleeping dogs lie. You forget all about it, destroy the intelligence analyzer, and I'll tell you what to use for a lamp filament.' "

"Hogwash!" said Bullard, his face purple.

The stranger stood. "You have my solemn word as a gentleman. That dog rewarded *me* for my silence with a stock-market tip that made me independently wealthy for the rest of my days. And the last words that Sparky ever spoke were to Thomas Edison. 'Try a piece of carbonized cotton thread,' he said. Later, he was torn to bits by a pack of dogs that had gathered outside the door, listening."

The stranger removed his garters and handed them to Bullard's dog. "A small token of esteem, sir, for an ancestor of yours who talked himself to death. Good day." He tucked his book under his arm and walked away. His step was brisk and spry as though the Florida sunshine were already working its magic.

Unready
to Wear

I DON'T suppose the oldsters, those of us who weren't born into it, will ever feel quite at home being amphibious —amphibious in the new sense of the word. I still catch myself feeling blue about things that don't matter any more.

I can't help worrying about my business, for instance —or what used to be my business. After all, I spent thirty years building the thing up from scratch, and now the equipment is rusting and getting clogged with dirt. But even though I know it's silly of me to care what happens to the business, I borrow a body from a storage center every so often, and go around the old home town, and clean and oil as much of the equipment as I can.

Of course, all in the world the equipment was good for was making money, and Lord knows there's plenty of that lying around. Not as much as there used to be, because there at first some people got frisky and threw it all around, and the wind blew it every which way. And a lot of go-getters gathered up piles of the stuff and hid it somewhere. I hate to admit it, but I gathered up close to a half million myself and stuck it away. I used to get it out and count it sometimes, but that was years ago. Right now I'd be hard put to say where it is.

But the worrying I do about my old business is bush league stuff compared to the worrying my wife, Madge, does about our old house. That thing is what she herself put in thirty years on while I was building the business. Then no sooner had we gotten nerve enough to build and decorate the place than everybody we cared anything about got amphibious. Madge borrows a body once a month and dusts the place, though the only thing a house is good for now is keeping termites and mice from getting pneumonia.

WHENEVER it's my turn to get into a body and work as an attendant at the local storage center, I realize all over again how much tougher it is for women to get used to being amphibious.

Madge borrows bodies a lot oftener than I do, and that's true of women in general. We have to keep three times as many women's bodies in stock as men's bodies, in order to meet the demand. Every so often, it seems as though a woman just *has* to have a body, and doll it up in clothes, and look at herself in a mirror. And Madge, God bless her, I don't think she'll be satisfied until she's tried on every body in every storage center on Earth.

It's been a fine thing for Madge, though. I never kid her about it, because it's done so much for her personality. Her old body, to tell you the plain blunt truth, wasn't anything to get excited about, and having to haul the thing around made her gloomy a lot of the time in the old days. She couldn't help it, poor soul, any more than anybody else could help what sort of body they'd been born with, and I loved her in spite of it.

Well, after we'd learned to be amphibious, and after we'd built the storage centers and laid in body supplies and opened them to the public, Madge went hog wild. She borrowed a platinum blonde body that had been donated by a burlesque queen, and I didn't think we'd ever get her out of it. As I say, it did wonders for her self-confidence.

I'm like most men and don't care particularly what body I get. Just the strong, good-looking, healthy bodies were put in storage, so one is as good as the next one. Sometimes, when Madge and I take bodies out together for old times' sake, I let her pick out one for me to match whatever she's got on. It's a funny thing how she always picks a blond, tall one for me.

My old body, which she claims she loved for a third of a century, had black hair, and was short and paunchy, too, there toward the last. I'm human and I couldn't help being hurt when they scrapped it after I'd left it, instead of putting it in storage. It was a good, homey, comfortable body; nothing fast and flashy, but reliable. But there isn't much call for that kind of body at the centers, I guess. I never ask for one, at any rate.

The worst experience I ever had with a body was when I was flimflammed into taking out the one that had belonged to Dr. Ellis Konigswasser. It belongs to the Amphibious Pioneers' Society and only gets taken out once a year for the big Pioneers' Day Parade, on the anniversary of Konigswasser's discovery. Everybody said it was a great honor for me to be picked to get into Konigswasser's body and lead the parade.

Like a plain damn fool, I believed them.

THEY'LL have a tough time getting me into that thing again—ever. Taking that wreck out certainly made it plain why Konigswasser discovered how people could do without their bodies. That old one of his practically *drives* you out. Ulcers, headaches, arthritis, fallen arches —a nose like a pruning hook, piggy little eyes, and a complexion like a used steamer trunk. He was and still is the sweetest person you'd ever want to know, but, back when he was stuck with that body, nobody got close enough to find out.

We tried to get Konigswasser back into his old body to lead us when we first started having the Pioneers' Day Parades, but he wouldn't have anything to do with it, so we always have to flatter some poor boob into taking on the job. Konigswasser marches, all right, but as a sixfoot cowboy who can bend beer cans double between his thumb and middle finger.

Konigswasser is just like a kid with that body. He never gets tired of bending beer cans with it, and we all have to stand around in our bodies after the parade, and watch as though we were very impressed.

I don't suppose he could bend very much of anything back in the old days.

Nobody mentions it to him, since he's the grand old man of the Amphibious Age, but he plays hell with bodies. Almost every time he takes one out, he busts it, showing off. Then somebody has to get into a surgeon's body and sew it up again.

I don't mean to be disrespectful of Konigswasser. As a matter of fact, it's a respectful thing to say that somebody is childish in certain ways, because it's people like that who seem to get all the big ideas.

There is a picture of him in the old days down at the Historical Society, and you can see from that that he never did grow up as far as keeping up his appearance went—doing what little he could with the rattle-trap body Nature had issued him.

His hair was down below his collar, he wore his pants so low that his heels wore through the legs above the cuffs, and the lining of his coat hung down in festoons all around the bottom. And he'd forget meals, and go out into the cold or wet without enough clothes on, and he would never notice sickness until it almost killed him. He was what we used to call absent-minded. Looking back now, of course, we say he was starting to be amphibious.

KONIGSWASSER was a mathematician, and he did all his living with his mind. The body he had to haul around with that wonderful mind was about as much use to him as a flatcar of scrap-iron. Whenever he got sick and *had* to pay some attention to his body, he'd rant somewhat like this:

"The mind is the only thing about human beings that's worth anything. Why does it have to be tied to a bag of skin, blood, hair, meat, bones, and tubes? No wonder people can't get anything done, stuck for life with a parasite that has to be stuffed with food and protected from weather and germs all the time. And the fool thing wears out anyway—no matter how much you stuff and protect it!

"Who," he wanted to know, "really wants one of the things? What's so wonderful about protoplasm that we've got to carry so damned many pounds of it with us wherever we go?

"Trouble with the world," said Konigswasser, "isn't too many people—it's too many bodies."

When his teeth went bad on him, and he had to have them all out, and he couldn't get a set of dentures that were at all comfortable, he wrote in his diary, "If living matter was able to evolve enough to get out of the ocean, which was really quite a pleasant place to live, it certainly ought to be able to take another step and get out of bodies, which are pure nuisances when you stop to think about them."

He wasn't a prude about bodies, understand, and he wasn't jealous of people who had better ones than he did. He just thought bodies were a lot more trouble than they were worth.

He didn't have great hopes that people would really evolve out of their bodies in his time. He just wished they would. Thinking hard about it, he walked through a park in his shirtsleeves and stopped off at the zoo to watch the lions being fed. Then, when the rainstorm turned to sleet, he headed back home and was interested to see firemen on the edge of a lagoon, where they were using a pulmotor on a drowned man.

Witnesses said the old man had walked right into the water and had kept going without changing his expression until he'd disappeared. Konigswasser got a look at the victim's face and said he'd never seen a better reason for suicide. He started for home again and was almost there before he realized that that was his own body lying back there.

He went back to reoccupy the body just as the firemen got it breathing again, and he walked it home, more as a favor to the city than anything else. He walked it into his front closet, got out of it again, and left it there.

He took it out only when he wanted to do some writing or turn the pages of a book, or when he had to feed it so it would have enough energy to do the few odd jobs he gave it. The rest of the time, it sat motionless in the closet, looking dazed and using almost no energy. Konigswasser told me the other day that he used to run the thing for about a dollar a week, just taking it out when he really needed it.

But the best part was that Konigswasser didn't have to sleep any more, just because *it* had to sleep; or be afraid any more, just because *it* thought it might get hurt; or go looking for things *it* seemed to think it had to have. And, when *it* didn't feel well, Konigswasser kept out of it until it felt better, and he didn't have to spend a fortune keeping the thing comfortable.

When he got his body out of the closet to write, he did a book on how to get out of one's own body, which was rejected without comment by twenty-three publishers. The twenty-fourth sold two million copies, and the book changed human life more than the invention of fire, numbers, the alphabet, agriculture, or the wheel. When somebody told Konigswasser that, he snorted that they were damning his book with faint praise. I'd say he had a point there.

By following the instructions in Konigswasser's book for about two years, almost anybody could get out of his body whenever he wanted to. The first step was to understand what a parasite and dictator the body was most of the time, then to separate what the body wanted or didn't want from what you yourself—your psyche—wanted or didn't want. Then, by concentrating on what you wanted, and ignoring as much as possible what the body wanted beyond plain maintenance, you made your psyche demand its rights and become self-sufficient.

That's what Konigswasser had done without realizing it, until he and his body had parted company in the park, with his psyche going to watch the lions eat, and with his body wandering out of control into the lagoon.

The final trick of separation, once your psyche grew independent enough, was to start your body walking into some direction and suddenly take your psyche off in another direction. You couldn't do it standing still, for some reason—you had to walk.

At first, Madge's and my psyches were clumsy at getting along outside our bodies, like the first sea animals that got stranded on land millions of years ago, and who could just waddle and squirm and gasp in the mud. But we became better at it with time, because the psyche can naturally adapt so much faster than the body.

MADGE and I had good reason for wanting to get out. Everybody who was crazy enough to try to get out at the first had good reasons. Madge's body was sick and wasn't going to last a lot longer. With her going in a little while, I couldn't work up enthusiasm for sticking around much longer myself. So we studied Konigswasser's book and tried to get Madge out of her body before it died. I went along with her, to keep either one of us from getting lonely. And we just barely made it—six weeks before her body went all to pieces.

That's why we get to march every year in the Pioneers' Day Parade. Not everybody does—only the first five thousand of us who turned amphibious. We were guinea pigs, without much to lose one way or another, and we were the ones who proved to the rest how pleasant and safe it was—a heck of a lot safer than taking chances in a body year in and year out.

Sooner or later, almost everybody had a good reason for giving it a try. There got to be millions and finally more than a billion of us—invisible, insubstantial, indestructible, and, by golly, true to ourselves, no trouble to anybody, and not afraid of anything.

When we're not in bodies, the Amphibious Pioneers can meet on the head of a pin. When we get into bodies for the Pioneers' Day Parade, we take up over fifty thousand square feet, have to gobble more than three tons of food to get enough energy to march; and lots of us catch colds or worse, and get sore because somebody's body accidentally steps on the heel of somebody else's body, and get jealous because some bodies get to lead and others have to stay in ranks, and—oh, hell, I don't know what all.

I'm not crazy about the parade. With all of us there, close together in bodies—well, it brings out the worst in us, no matter how good our psyches are. Last year, for instance, Pioneers' Day was a scorcher. People couldn't help being out of sorts, stuck in sweltering, thirsty bodies for hours.

Well, one thing led to another, and the Parade Marshal offered to beat the daylights out of my body with his body, if my body got out of step again. Naturally, being Parade Marshal, he had the best body that year, except for Konigswasser's cowboy, but I told him to soak his fat head, anyway. He swung, and I ditched my body right there, and didn't even stick around long enough to find out if he connected. He had to haul my body back to the storage center himself.

I stopped being mad at him the minute I got out of the body. I understood, you see. Nobody but a saint could be really sympathetic or intelligent for more than a few minutes at a time in a body—or happy, either, except in short spurts. I haven't met an amphibian yet who wasn't easy to get along with, and cheerful and interesting—as long as he was outside a body. And I haven't met one yet who didn't turn a little sour when he got into one.

The minute you get in, chemistry takes over—glands making you excitable or ready to fight or hungry or mad or affectionate, or—well, you never know *what's* going to happen next.

THAT'S why I can't get sore at the enemy, the people who are against the amphibians. They never get out of their bodies and won't try to learn. They don't want anybody else to do it, either, and they'd like to make the amphibians get back into bodies and stay in them.

After the tussle I had with the Parade Marshal, Madge got wind of it and left *her* body right in the middle of the Ladies' Auxiliary. And the two of us, feeling full of devilment after getting shed of the bodies and the parade, went over to have a look at the enemy.

I'm never keen on going over to look at them. Madge likes to see what the women are wearing. Stuck with their bodies all the time, the enemy women change their clothes and hair and cosmetic styles a lot oftener than we do on the women's bodies in the storage centers.

I don't get much of a kick out of the fashions, and almost everything else you see and hear in enemy territory would bore a plaster statue into moving away.

Usually, the enemy is talking about old-style reproduction, which is the clumsiest, most comical, most inconvenient thing anyone could imagine, compared with what the amphibians have in that line. If they aren't talking about that, then they're talking about food, the gobs of chemicals they have to stuff into their bodies. Or they'll talk about fear, which we used to call politics—job politics, social politics, government politics.

The enemy hates that, having us able to peek in on them any time we want to, while they can't ever see us unless we get into bodies. They seem to be scared to death of us, though being scared of amphibians makes as much sense as being scared of the sunrise. They could have the whole world, except the storage centers, for all the amphibians care. But they bunch together as though we were going to come whooping out of the sky and do something terrible to them at any moment.

They've got contraptions all over the place that are supposed to detect amphibians. The gadgets aren't worth a nickel, but they seem to make the enemy feel good— like they were lined up against great forces, but keeping their nerve and doing important, clever things about it. Knowhow—all the time they're patting each other about how much knowhow they've got, and about how we haven't got anything by comparison. If knowhow means weapons, they're dead right.

I GUESS there is a war on between them and us. But we never do anything about holding up our side of the war, except to keep our parade sites and our storage centers secret, and to get out of bodies every time there's an air raid, or the enemy fires a rocket, or something.

That just makes the enemy madder, because the raids and rockets and all cost plenty, and blowing up things nobody needs anyway is a poor return on the taxpayer's money. We always know what they're going to do next, and when and where, so there isn't any trick to keeping out of their way.

But they are pretty smart, considering they've got bodies to look after besides doing their thinking, so I always try to be cautious when I go over to watch them. That's why I wanted to clear out when Madge and I saw a storage center in the middle of one of their fields. We hadn't talked to anybody lately about what the enemy was up to, and the center looked awfully suspicious.

Madge was optimistic, the way she's been ever since she borrowed that burlesque queen's body, and she said the storage center was a sure sign that the enemy had seen the light, that they were getting ready to become amphibious themselves.

Well, it looked like it. There was a brand-new center, stocked with bodies and open for business, as innocent as you please. We circled it several times, and Madge's circles got smaller and smaller, as she tried to get a close look at what they had in the way of ladies' ready-to-wear.

"Let's beat it," I said.

"I'm just looking," said Madge. "No harm in looking."

Then she saw what was in the main display case, and she forgot where she was or where she'd come from.

The most striking woman's body I'd ever seen was in the case—six feet tall and built like a goddess. But that wasn't the payoff. The body had copper-colored skin, chartreuse hair and fingernails, and a gold lamé evening gown. Beside that body was the body of a blond, male giant in a pale blue field marshal's uniform, piped in scarlet, and spangled with medals.

I think the enemy must have swiped the bodies in a raid on one of our outlying storage centers, and padded and dyed them, and dressed them up.

"Madge, come back!" I said.

The copper-colored woman with the chartreuse hair moved. A siren screamed and soldiers rushed from hiding places to grab the body Madge was in.

The center was a trap for amphibians!

The body Madge hadn't been able to resist had its ankles tied together, so Madge couldn't take the few steps she had to take if she was going to get out of it again.

The soldiers carted her off triumphantly as a prisoner of war. I got into the only body available, the fancy field marshal, to try to help her. It was a hopeless situation, because the field marshal was bait, too, with its ankles tied. The soldiers dragged me after Madge.

THE cocky young major in charge of the soldiers did a jig along the shoulder of the road, he was so proud. He was the first man ever to capture an amphibian, which was really something from the enemy's point of view. They'd been at war with us for years, and spent God knows how many billions of dollars, but catching us was the first thing that made any amphibians pay much attention to them.

When we got to the town, people were leaning out of windows and waving their flags, and cheering the soldiers, and hissing Madge and me. Here were all the people who didn't want to be amphibious, who thought it was terrible for anybody to be amphibious—people of all colors, shapes, sizes, and nationalities, joined together to fight the amphibians.

It turned out that Madge and I were going to have a big trial. After being tied up every which way in jail all night, we were taken to a court room, where television cameras stared at us.

Madge and I were worn to frazzles, because neither one of us had been cooped up in a body that long since I don't know when. Just when we needed to think more than we ever had, in jail before the trial, the bodies developed hunger pains and we couldn't get them comfortable on the cots, no matter how we tried; and, of course, the bodies just had to have their eight hours sleep.

The charge against us was a capital offense on the books of the enemy—*desertion*. As far as the enemy was concerned, the amphibians had all turned yellow and run out on their bodies, just when their bodies were needed to do brave and important things for humanity.

We didn't have a hope of being acquitted. The only reason there was a trial at all was that it gave them an opportunity to sound off about why they were so right and we were so wrong. The court room was jammed with their big brass, all looking angry and brave and noble.

"Mr. Amphibian," said the prosecutor, "you are old enough, aren't you, to remember when all men had to face up to life in their bodies, and work and fight for what they believed in?"

"I remember when the bodies were always getting into fights, and nobody seemed to know why, or how to stop it," I said politely. "The only thing everybody seemed to believe in was that they didn't like to fight."

"What would you say of a soldier who ran away in the face of fire?" he wanted to know.

"I'd say he was scared silly."

"He was helping to lose the battle, wasn't he?"

"Oh, sure." There wasn't any argument on that one.

"Isn't that what the amphibians have done—run out on the human race in the face of the battle of life?"

"Most of us are still alive, if that's what you mean," I said.

IT was true. We hadn't licked death, and weren't sure we wanted to, but we'd certainly lengthened life something amazing, compared to the span you could expect in a body.

"You ran out on your responsibilities!" he said.

"Like you'd run out of a burning building, sir," I said.

"Leaving everyone else to struggle on alone!"

"They can all get out the same door that we got out of. You can all get out any time you want to. All you do is figure out what you want and what your body wants, and concentrate on—"

The judge banged his gavel until I thought he'd split it. Here they'd burned every copy of Konigswasser's book they could find, and there I was giving a course in how to get out of a body over a whole television network.

"If you amphibians had your way," said the prosecutor, "everybody would run out on his responsibilities, and let life and progress as we know them disappear completely."

"Why, sure," I agreed. "That's the point."

"Men would no longer work for what they believe in?" he challenged.

"I had a friend back in the old days who drilled holes in little square thingamajigs for seventeen years in a factory, and he never did get a very clear idea of what they were for. Another one I knew grew raisins for a glassblowing company, and the raisins weren't for anybody to eat, and he never did find out why the company bought them. Things like that make me sick—now that I'm in a body, of course—and what I used to do for a living makes me even sicker."

"Then you despise human beings and everything they do," he said.

"I like them fine—better than I ever did before. I just think it's a dirty shame what they have to do to take care of their bodies. You ought to get amphibious and see how happy people can be when they don't have to worry about where their body's next meal is coming from, or how to keep it from freezing in the wintertime, or what's going to happen to them when their body wears out."

"And that, sir, means the end of ambition, the end of greatness!"

"Oh, I don't know about that," I said. "We've got some pretty great people on our side. They'd be great in *or* out of bodies. It's the end of fear is what it is." I looked right into the lens of the nearest television camera. "And *that's* the most wonderful thing that ever happened to people."

Down came the judge's gavel again, and the brass started to shout me down. The television men turned off their cameras, and all the spectators, except for the biggest brass, were cleared out. I knew I'd really said something. All anybody would be getting on his television set now was organ music.

When the confusion died down, the judge said the trial was over, and that Madge and I were guilty of desertion.

NOTHING I could do could get us in any worse, so I talked back.

"Now I understand you poor fish," I said. "You couldn't get along without fear. That's the only skill you've got—how to scare yourselves and other people into doing things. That's the only fun you've got, watching people jump for fear of what you'll do to their bodies or take away from their bodies."

Madge got in her two cents' worth. "The only way you can get any response from anybody is to scare them."

"Contempt of court!" said the judge.

"The only way you can scare people is if you can keep them in their bodies," I told him.

The soldiers grabbed Madge and me and started to drag us out of the court room.

"This means war!" I yelled.

Everything stopped right there and the place got very quiet.

"We're already at war," said a general uneasily.

"Well, *we're* not," I answered, "but we will be, if you don't untie Madge and me this instant." I was fierce and impressive in that field marshal's body.

"You haven't any weapons," said the judge, "no know-how. Outside of bodies, amphibians are nothing."

"If you don't cut us loose by the time I count ten," I told him, "the amphibians will occupy the bodies of the whole kit and caboodle of you and march you right off the nearest cliff. The place is surrounded." That was hogwash, of course. Only one person can occupy a body at a time, but the enemy couldn't be sure of that. "One! Two! Three!"

The general swallowed, turned white, and waved his hand vaguely.

"Cut them loose," he said weakly.

The soldiers, terrified, too, were glad to do it. Madge and I were freed.

I took a couple of steps, headed my spirit in another direction, and that beautiful field marshal, medals and all, went crashing down the staircase like a grandfather clock.

I realized that Madge wasn't with me. She was still in that copper-colored body with the chartreuse hair and fingernails.

"What's more," I heard her saying, "in payment for all the trouble you've caused us, this body is to be addressed to me at New York, delivered in good condition no later than next Monday."

"Yes, ma'am," said the judge.

When we got home, the Pioneers' Day Parade was just breaking up at the local storage center, and the Parade Marshal got out of his body and apologized to me for acting the way he had.

"Heck, Herb," I said, "you don't need to apologize. You weren't yourself. You were parading around in a body."

That's the best part of being amphibious, next to not being afraid—people forgive you for whatever fool thing you might have done in a body.

Oh, there are drawbacks, I guess, the way there are drawbacks to everything. We still have to work off and on, maintaining the storage centers and getting food to keep the community bodies going. But that's a small drawback, and all the big drawbacks I ever heard of aren't real ones, just old-fashioned thinking by people who can't stop worrying about things they used to worry about before they turned amphibious.

As I say, the oldsters will probably never get really used to it. Every so often, I catch myself getting gloomy over what happened to the pay-toilet business it took me thirty years to build.

But the youngsters don't have any hangovers like that from the past. They don't even worry much about something happening to the storage centers, the way us oldsters do.

So I guess maybe that'll be the next step in evolution—
to break clean like those first amphibians who crawled
out of the mud into the sunshine, and who never did go
back to the sea.

Tomorrow and Tomorrow and Tomorrow

THE year was 2158 A.D., and Lou and Emerald Schwartz were whispering on the balcony outside of Lou's family's apartment on the 76th floor of Building 257 in Alden Village, a New York housing development that covered what had once been known as Southern Connecticut. When Lou and Emerald had married, Em's parents had tearfully described the marriage as being between May and December; but now, with Lou 112 and Em 93, Em's parents had to admit that the match had worked out surprisingly well.

But Em and Lou weren't without their troubles, and they were out in the nippy air of the balcony because of them. What they were saying was bitter and private.

"Sometimes I get so mad, I feel like just up and diluting his anti-gerasone," said Em.

"That'd be against Nature, Em," said Lou, "it'd be murder. Besides, if he caught us tinkering with his anti-gerasone, not only would he disinherit us, he'd bust my

146

neck. Just because he's 172 doesn't mean Gramps isn't strong as a bull."

"Against Nature," said Em. "Who knows what Nature's like anymore? Ohhhhh—I don't guess I could ever bring myself to dilute his anti-gerasone or anything like that, but, gosh, Lou, a body can't help thinking Gramps is never going to leave if somebody doesn't help him along a little. Golly—we're so crowded a person can hardly turn around, and Verna's dying for a baby, and Melissa's gone thirty years without one." She stamped her feet. "I get so sick of seeing his wrinkled old face, watching him take the only private room and the best chair and the best food, and getting to pick out what to watch on TV, and running everybody's life by changing his will all the time."

"Well, after all," said Lou bleakly, "Gramps *is* head of the family. And he can't help being wrinkled like he is. He was 70 before anti-gerasone was invented. He's going to leave, Em. Just give him time. It's his business. I know he's tough to live with, but be patient. It wouldn't do to do anything that'd rile him. After all, we've got it better'n anybody else, there on the daybed."

"How much longer do you think we'll get to sleep on the daybed before he picks another pet? The world's record's two months, isn't it?"

"Mom and Pop had it that long once, I guess."

"When *is* he going to leave, Lou?" said Emerald.

"Well, he's talking about giving up anti-gerasone right after the 500-mile Speedway Race."

"Yes—and before that it was the Olympics, and before that the World's Series, and before that the Presidential Elections, and before that I-don't-know-what. It's been just one excuse after another for 50 years now. I don't think we're ever going to get a room to ourselves or an egg or anything."

"All right—call me a failure!" said Lou. "What can I do? I work hard and make good money, but the whole thing, practically, is taxed away for defense and old age pensions. And if it wasn't taxed away, where you think we'd find a vacant room to rent? Iowa, maybe? Well, who wants to live on the outskirts of Chicago?"

Em put her arms around his neck. "Lou, hon, I'm not calling you a failure. The Lord knows you're not. You just haven't had a chance to be anything or have anything because Gramps and the rest of his generation won't leave and let somebody else take over."

"Yeah, yeah," said Lou gloomily. "You can't exactly blame 'em, though, can you? I mean, I wonder how quick we'll knock off the anti-gerasone when we get Gramps' age."

"Sometimes I wish there wasn't any such thing as anti-gerasone!" said Emerald passionately. "Or I wish it was made out of something real expensive and hard-to-get instead of mud and dandelions. Sometimes I wish folks just up and died regular as clockwork, without anything to say about it, instead of deciding themselves how long they're going to stay around. There ought to be a law against selling the stuff to anybody over 150."

"Fat chance of that," said Lou, "with all the money and votes the old people've got." He looked at her closely. "You ready to up and die, Em?"

"Well, for heaven's sakes, what a thing to say to your wife. Hon! I'm not even 100 yet." She ran her hands lightly over her firm, youthful figure, as though for confirmation. "The best years of my life are still ahead of me. But you can bet that when 150 rolls around, old Em's going to pour her anti-gerasone down the sink, and quit taking up room, and she'll do it smiling."

"Sure, sure," said Lou, "you bet. That's what they all say. How many you heard of doing it?"

"There was that man in Delaware."

"Aren't you getting kind of tired of talking about him, Em? That was five months ago."

"All right, then—Gramma Winkler, right here in the same building."

"She got smeared by a subway."

"That's just the way she picked to go," said Em.

"Then what was she doing carrying a carton of anti-gerasone when she got it?"

Emerald shook her head wearily and covered her eyes. "I dunno, I dunno, I dunno. All I know is, something's just got to be done." She sighed. "Sometimes I wish they'd left a couple of diseases kicking around somewhere, so I could get one and go to bed for a little while. Too many people!" she cried, and her words cackled and gabbled and died in a thousand asphalt-paved, skyscraper-walled courtyards.

Lou laid his hand on her shoulder tenderly. "Aw, hon, I hate to see you down in the dumps like this."

"If we just had a car, like the folks used to in the old days," said Em, "we could go for a drive, and get away from people for a little while. Gee—if *those* weren't the days!"

"Yeah," said Lou, "before they'd used up all the metal."

"We'd hop in, and Pop'd drive up to a filling station and say, 'Fillerup!' "

"That *was* the nuts, wasn't it—before they'd used up all the gasoline."

"And we'd go for a carefree ride in the country."

"Yeah—all seems like a fairyland now, doesn't it, Em? Hard to believe there really used to be all that space between cities."

"And when we got hungry," said Em, "we'd find ourselves a restaurant, and walk in, big as you please and say, 'I'll have a steak and French-fries, I believe,' or, 'How are the pork chops today?' " She licked her lips, and her eyes glistened.

"Yeah man!" growled Lou. "How'd you like a hamburger with the works, Em?"

"Mmmmmmmm."

"If anybody'd offered us processed seaweed in those days, we would have spit right in his eye, huh, Em?"

"Or processed sawdust," said Em.

Doggedly, Lou tried to find the cheery side of the situation. "Well, anyway, they've got the stuff so it tastes a lot less like seaweed and sawdust than it did at first; and they say it's actually better for us than what we used to eat."

"I felt fine!" said Em fiercely.

Lou shrugged. "Well, you've got to realize, the world wouldn't be able to support twelve billion people if it wasn't for processed seaweed and sawdust. I mean, it's a wonderful thing, really. I guess. That's what they say."

"They say the first thing that pops into their heads," said Em. She closed her eyes. "Golly—remember shopping, Lou? Remember how the stores used to fight to get our folks to buy something? You didn't have to wait for somebody to die to get a bed or chairs or a stove or anything like that. Just went in—bing!—and bought whatever you wanted. Gee whiz that was nice, before they used up all the raw materials. I was just a little kid then, but I can remember so plain."

Depressed, Lou walked listlessly to the balcony's edge, and looked up at the clean, cold, bright stars against the black velvet of infinity. "Remember when we used to be bugs on science fiction, Em? Flight seventeen, leaving for Mars, launching ramp twelve. 'Board! All non-technical personnel kindly remain in bunkers. Ten seconds . . . nine . . . eight . . . seven . . . six . . . five . . . four . . . three . . . two . . . one! *Main Stage! Barrrrrroooom!*"

"Why worry about what was going on on Earth?" said Em, looking up at the stars with him. "In another few years, we'd all be shooting through space to start life all over again on a new planet."

Lou sighed. "Only it turns out you need something about twice the size of the Empire State Building to get one lousy colonist to Mars. And for another couple of trillion bucks he could take his wife and dog. *That's* the way to lick overpopulation—*emigrate!*"

"Lou—?"

"Hmmm?"

"When's the 500-mile Speedway Race?"

"Uh—Memorial Day, May 30th."

She bit her lip. "Was that awful of me to ask?"

"Not very, I guess. Everybody in the apartment's looked it up to make sure."

"I don't want to be awful," said Em, "but you've just got to talk over these things now and then, and get them out of your system."

"Sure you do. Feel better?"

"Yes—and I'm not going to lose my temper anymore, and I'm going to be just as nice to him as I know how."

"That's my Em."

They squared their shoulders, smiled bravely, and went back inside.

GRAMPS SCHWARTZ, his chin resting on his hands, his hands on the crook of his cane, was staring irascibly at the five-foot television screen that dominated the room. On the screen, a news commentator was summarizing the day's happenings. Every thirty seconds or so, Gramps would jab the floor with his canetip and shout, "Hell! We did that a hundred years ago!"

Emerald and Lou, coming in from the balcony, were

obliged to take seats in the back row, behind Lou's
father and mother, brother and sister-in-law, son and
daughter-in-law, grandson and wife, granddaughter and
husband, great-grandson and wife, nephew and wife
grandnephew and wife, great-grandniece and husband,
great-grandnephew and wife, and, of course, Gramps,
who was in front of everybody. All, save Gramps, who
was somewhat withered and bent, seemed, by pre-anti-
gerasone standards, to be about the same age—to be
somewhere in their late twenties or early thirties.

"Meanwhile," the commentator was saying, *"Council
Bluffs, Iowa, was still threatened by stark tragedy. But
200 weary rescue workers have refused to give up hope,
and continue to dig in an effort to save Elbert Haggedorn,
183, who has been wedged for two days in a . . ."*

"I wish he'd get something more cheerful," Emerald
whispered to Lou.

"Silence!" cried Gramps. "Next one shoots off his big
bazoo while the TV's on is gonna find hisself cut off
without a dollar—" and here his voice suddenly softened
and sweetened—"when they wave that checkered flag at
the Indianapolis Speedway, and old Gramps gets ready
for the Big Trip Up Yonder." He sniffed sentimentally,
while his heirs concentrated desperately on not making
the slightest sound. For them, the poignancy of the prospective Big Trip had been dulled somewhat by its having
been mentioned by Gramps about once a day for fifty
years.

"Dr. Brainard Keyes Bullard," said the commentator,
*"President of Wyandotte College, said in an address to-
night that most of the world's ills can be traced to the fact
that Man's knowledge of himself has not kept pace with
his knowledge of the physical world."*

"Hell!" said Gramps. "We said that a hundred years
ago!"

"In Chicago tonight," said the commentator, *"a special
celebration is taking place in the Chicago Lying-in Hospital. The guest of honor is Lowell W. Hitz, age zero.
Hitz, born this morning, is the twenty-five millionth child
to be born in the hospital."* The commentator faded, and
was replaced on the screen by young Hitz, who squalled
furiously.

"Hell," whispered Lou to Emerald, "we said that a
hundred years ago."

"I heard that!" shouted Gramps. He snapped off the television set, and his petrified descendants stared silently at the screen. "You, there, boy—"

"I didn't mean anything by it, sir," said Lou.

"Get me my will. You know where it is. You kids *all* know where it is. Fetch, boy!"

Lou nodded dully, and found himself going down the hall, picking his way over bedding to Gramps' room, the only private room in the Schwartz apartment. The other rooms were the bathroom, the livingroom, and the wide, windowless hallway, which was originally intended to serve as a dining area, and which had a kitchenette in one end. Six mattresses and four sleeping bags were dispersed in the hallway and livingroom, and the daybed, in the livingroom, accommodated the eleventh couple, the favorites of the moment.

On Gramps' bureau was his will, smeared, dog-eared, perforated, and blotched with hundreds of additions, deletions, accusations, conditions, warnings, advice, and homely philosophy. The document was, Lou reflected, a fifty-year diary, all jammed onto two sheets—a garbled, illegible log of day after day of strife. This day, Lou would be disinherited for the eleventh time, and it would take him perhaps six months of impeccable behavior to regain the promise of a share in the estate.

"Boy!" called Gramps.

"Coming, sir." Lou hurried back into the livingroom, and handed Gramps the will.

"Pen!" said Gramps.

He was instantly offered eleven pens, one from each couple.

"Not *that* leaky thing," he said, brushing Lou's pen aside. "Ah, there's a nice one. Good boy, Willy." He accepted Willy's pen, That was the tip they'd all been waiting for. Willy, then, Lou's father, was the new favorite.

Willy, who looked almost as young as Lou, though 142, did a poor job of concealing his pleasure. He glanced shyly at the daybed, which would become his, and from which Lou and Emerald would have to move back into the hall, back to the worst spot of all by the bathroom door.

Gramps missed none of the high drama he'd authored, and he gave his own familiar role everything he had.

Frowning and running his finger along each line, as though he were seeing the will for the first time, he read aloud in a deep, portentous monotone, like a base tone on a cathedral organ:

"I, Harold D. Schwartz, residing in Building 257 of Alden Village, New York City, do hereby make, publish and declare this to be my last Will and Testament, hereby revoking any and all former wills and codicils by me at any time heretofore made." He blew his nose importantly, and went on, not missing a word, and repeating many for emphasis—repeating in particular his ever-more-elaborate specifications for a funeral.

At the end of these specifications, Gramps was so choked with emotion that Lou thought he might forget why he'd gotten out the will in the first place. But Gramps heroically brought his powerful emotions under control, and, after erasing for a full minute, he began to write and speak at the same time. Lou could have spoken his lines for him, he'd heard them so often.

"I have had many heartbreaks ere leaving this vale of tears for a better land," Gramps said and wrote. "But the deepest hurt of all has been dealt me by—" He looked around the group, trying to remember who the malefactor was.

Everyone looked helpfully at Lou, who held up his hand resignedly.

Gramps nodded, remembering, and completed the sentence: "my great-grandson, Louis J. Schwartz."

"Grandson, sir," said Lou.

"Don't quibble. You're in deep enough now, young man," said Gramps, but he changed the trifle. And from there he went without a mis-step through the phrasing of the disinheritance, causes for which were disrespectfulness and quibbling.

In the paragraph following, the paragraph that had belonged to everyone in the room at one time or another, Lou's name was scratched out and Willy's substituted as heir to the apartment and, the biggest plum of all, the double bed in the private bedroom. "So!" said Gramps, beaming. He erased the date at the foot of the will, and substituted a new one, including the time of day. "Well—time to watch the McGarvey Family." The McGarvey Family was a television serial that Gramps had been following since he was 60, or for 112 years. "I can't wait to see what's going to happen next," he said.

Lou detached himself from the group, and lay down on his bed of pain by the bathroom door. He wished Em would join him, and he wondered where she was.

He dozed for a few moments, until he was disturbed by someone's stepping over him to get into the bathroom. A moment later, he heard a faint gurgling sound, as though something were being poured down the washbasin drain. Suddenly, it entered his mind that Em had cracked up, and that she was in there doing something drastic about Gramps.

"Em—?" he whispered through the panel. There was no reply, and Lou pressed against the door. The worn lock, whose bolt barely engaged its socket, held for a second, then let the door swing inward.

"Morty!" gasped Lou.

Lou's great-grandnephew, Mortimer, who had just married and brought his wife home to the Schwartz menage, looked at Lou with consternation and surprise. Morty kicked the door shut, but not before Lou had glimpsed what was in his hand—Gramps' enormous economy-size bottle of anti-gerasone, which had been half-emptied, and which Morty was refilling to the top with tap water.

A moment later, Morty came out, glared defiantly at Lou, and brushed past him wordlessly to rejoin his pretty bride.

Shocked, Lou didn't know what on earth to do. He couldn't let Gramps take the mouse-trapped anti-gerasone; but if he warned Gramps about it, Gramps would certainly make life in the apartment, which was merely insufferable now, harrowing.

Lou glanced into the livingroom, and saw that the Schwartzes, Emerald among them, were momentarily at rest, relishing the botches that the McGarveys had made of *their* lives. Stealthily, he went into the bathroom, locked the door as well as he could, and began to pour the contents of Gramps' bottle down the drain. He was going to refill it with full-strength anti-gerasone from the 22 smaller bottles on the shelf. The bottle contained a half-gallon, and its neck was small, so it seemed to Lou that the emptying would take forever. And the almost imperceptible smell of anti-gerasone, like Worcestershire sauce, now seemed to Lou, in his nervousness, to be pouring out into the rest of the apartment through the keyhole and under the door.

"Gloog-gloog-gloog-gloog-," went the bottle monotonously. Suddenly, up came the sound of music from the livingroom, and there were murmurs and the scraping of chairlegs on the floor. *"Thus ends,"* said the television announcer, *"the 29,121st chapter in the life of your neighbors and mine, the McGarveys."* Footsteps were coming down the hall. There was a knock on the bathroom door.

"Just a sec," called Lou cheerily. Desperately, he shook the big bottle, trying to speed up the flow. His palms slipped on the wet glass, and the heavy bottle smashed to splinters on the tile floor.

The door sprung open, and Gramps, dumbfounded, stared at the incriminating mess.

Lou felt a hideous prickling sensation on his scalp and the back of his neck. He grinned engagingly through his nausea, and, for want of anything remotely resembling a thought, he waited for Gramps to speak.

"Well, boy," said Gramps at last, "looks like you've got a little tidying up to do."

And that was all he said. He turned around, elbowed his way through the crowd, and locked himself in his bedroom.

The Schwartzes contemplated Lou in incredulous silence for a moment longer, and then hurried back to the livingroom, as though some of his horrible guilt would taint them, too, if they looked too long. Morty stayed behind long enough to give Lou a quizzical, annoyed glance. Then he, too, went into the livingroom, leaving only Emerald standing in the doorway.

Tears streamed over her cheeks. "Oh, you poor lamb— please don't look so awful. It was my fault. I put you up to this."

"No," said Lou, finding his voice, "really you didn't. Honest, Em, I was just—"

"You don't have to explain anything to me, hon. I'm on your side no matter what." She kissed him on his cheek, and whispered in his ear. "It wouldn't have been murder, hon. It wouldn't have killed him. It wasn't such a terrible thing to do. It just would have fixed him up so he'd be able to go any time God decided He wanted him."

"What's gonna happen next, Em?" said Lou hollowly. "What's he gonna do?"

Lou and Emerald stayed fearfully awake almost all night, waiting to see what Gramps was going to do. But not a sound came from the sacred bedroom. At two hours before dawn, the pair dropped off to sleep.

At six o'clock they arose again, for it was time for their generation to eat breakfast in the kitchenette. No one spoke to them. They had twenty minutes in which to eat, but their reflexes were so dulled by the bad night that they had hardly swallowed two mouthfuls of egg-type processed seaweed before it was time to surrender their places to their son's generation.

Then, as was the custom for whomever had been most recently disinherited, they began preparing Gramps' breakfast, which would presently be served to him in bed, on a tray. They tried to be cheerful about it. The toughest part of the job was having to handle the honest-to-God eggs and bacon and oleomargarine on which Gramps spent almost all of the income from his fortune.

"Well," said Emerald, "I'm not going to get all panicky until I'm sure there's something to be panicky about."

"Maybe he doesn't know what it was I busted," said Lou hopefully.

"Probably thinks it was your watch crystal," said Eddie, their son, who was toying apathetically with his buckwheat-type processed sawdust cakes.

"Don't get sarcastic with your father," said Em, "and don't talk with your mouth full, either."

"I'd like to see anybody take a mouthful of this stuff and *not* say something," said Eddie, who was 73. He glanced at the clock. "It's time to take Gramps his breakfast, you know."

"Yeah, it is, isn't it," said Lou weakly. He shrugged. "Let's have the tray, Em."

"We'll both go."

Walking slowly, smiling bravely, they found a large semi-circle of long-faced Schwartzes standing around the bedroom door.

Em knocked. "Gramps," she said brightly, "break-fast is rea-dy."

There was no reply, and she knocked again, harder. The door swung open before her fist. In the middle of the room, the soft, deep, wide, canopied bed, the symbol of the sweet by-and-by to every Schwartz, was empty.

A sense of death, as unfamiliar to the Schwartzes as Zoroastrianism or the causes of the Sepoy Mutiny, stilled every voice and slowed every heart. Awed, the heirs began to search gingerly under the furniture and behind the drapes for all that was mortal of Gramps, father of the race.

But Gramps had left not his earthly husk but a note, which Lou finally found on the dresser, under a paper-weight which was a treasured souvenir from the 2000 World's Fair. Unsteadily, Lou read it aloud:

" 'Somebody who I have sheltered and protected and taught the best I know how all these years last night turned on me like a mad dog and diluted my anti-gerasone, or tried to. I am no longer a young man. I can no longer bear the crushing burden of life as I once could. So, after last night's bitter experience, I say goodbye. The cares of this world will soon drop away like a cloak of thorns, and I shall know peace. By the time you find this, I will be gone.' "

"Gosh," said Willy brokenly, "he didn't even get to see how the 500-mile Speedway Race was going to come out."

"Or the World's Series," said Eddie.

"Or whether Mrs. McGarvey got her eyesight back," said Morty.

"There's more," said Lou, and he began reading aloud again: " 'I, Harold D. Schwartz . . . do hereby make, publish and declare this to be my last Will and Testament, hereby revoking any and all former will and codicils by me at any time heretofore made.' "

"No!" cried Willy. "Not another one!"

" 'I do stipulate,' " read Lou, " 'that all of my property, of whatsoever kind and nature, not be divided, but do devise and bequeath it to be held in common by my issue, without regard for generation, equally, share and share alike.' "

"Issue?" said Emerald.

Lou included the multitude in a sweep of his hand. "It means we all own the whole damn shootin' match."

All eyes turned instantly to the bed.

"Share and share alike?" said Morty.

"Actually," said Willy, who was the oldest person present, "it's just like the old system, where the oldest people head up things with their headquarters in here, and—"

"I like *that*!" said Em. "Lou owns as much of it as you do, and I say it ought to be for the oldest one who's still working. You can snooze around here all day, waiting for your pension check, and poor Lou stumbles in here after work, all tuckered out, and—"

"How about letting somebody who's never had any privacy get a little crack at it?" said Eddie hotly. "Hell, you old people had plenty of privacy back when you were kids. I was born and raised in the middle of the goddam barracks in the hall! How about—"

"Yeah?" said Morty. "Sure, you've all had it pretty tough, and my heart bleeds for you. But try honeymooning in the hall for a real kick."

"Silence!" shouted Willy imperiously. "The next person who opens his mouth spends the next six months by the bathroom. Now clear out of my room. I want to think."

A vase shattered against the wall, inches above his head. In the next moment, a free-for-all was underway, with each couple battling to eject every other couple from the room. Fighting coalitions formed and dissolved with the lightning changes of the tactical situation. Em and Lou were thrown into the hall, where they organized others in the same situation, and stormed back into the room.

After two hours of struggle, with nothing like a decision in sight, the cops broke in.

For the next half-hour, patrol wagons and ambulances hauled away Schwartzes, and then the apartment was still and spacious.

An hour later, films of the last stages of the riot were being televised to 500,000,000 delighted viewers on the Eastern Seaboard.

In the stillness of the three-room Schwartz apartment on the 76th floor of Building 257, the television set had been left on. Once more the air was filled with the cries and grunts and crashes of the fray, coming harmlessly now from the loudspeaker.

The battle also appeared on the screen of the television set in the police station, where the Schwartzes and their captors watched with professional interest.

Em and Lou were in adjacent four-by-eight cells, and were stretched out peacefully on their cots.

"Em—" called Lou through the partition, "you got a washbasin all your own too?"

"Sure. Washbasin, bed, light—the works. Ha! And we thought Gramps' room was something. How long's this been going on?" She held out her hand. "For the first time in forty years, hon, I haven't got the shakes."

"Cross your fingers;" said Lou, "the lawyer's going to try to get us a year."

"Gee," said Em dreamily, "I wonder what kind of wires you'd have to pull to get solitary?"

"All right, pipe down," said the turnkey, "or I'll toss the whole kit and caboodle of you right out. And first one who lets on to anybody outside how good jail is ain't never getting back in!"

The prisoners instantly fell silent.

The livingroom of the Schwartz apartment darkened for a moment, as the riot scenes faded, and then the face of the announcer appeared, like the sun coming from behind a cloud. *"And now, friends,"* he said, *"I have a special message from the makers of anti-gerasone, a message for all you folks over 150. Are you hampered socially by wrinkles, by stiffness of joints and discoloration or loss of hair, all because these things came upon you before anti-gerasone was developed? Well, if you are, you need no longer suffer, need no longer feel different and out of things.*

"After years of research, medical science has now developed super-anti-gerasone! In weeks, yes weeks, you can look, feel, and act as young as your great-great-grandchildren! Wouldn't you pay $5,000 to be indistinguishable from everybody else? Well, you don't have to. Safe, tested super-anti-gerasone costs you only dollars a day. The average cost of regaining all the sparkle and attractiveness of youth is less than fifty dollars.

"Write now for your free trial carton. Just put your name and address on a dollar postcard, and mail it to 'Super', Box 500,000, Schenectady, N. Y. Have you got that? I'll repeat it. 'Super,' Box . . ." Underlining the announcer's words was the scratching of Gramps' fountain-pen, the one Willy had given him the night before. He had come in a few minutes previous from the Idle Hour Tavern, which commanded a view of Building 257

across the square of asphalt known as the Alden Village Green. He had called a cleaning woman to come straighten the place up, and had hired the best lawyer in town to get his descendants a conviction. Gramps had then moved the daybed before the television screen so that he could watch from a reclining position. It was something he'd dreamed of doing for years.

"Schen-*ec*-ta-dy," mouthed Gramps. "Got it." His face had changed remarkably. His facial muscles seemed to have relaxed, revealing kindness and equanimity under what had been taut, bad-tempered lines. It was almost as though his trial package of *Super*-anti-gerasone had already arrived. When something amused him on television, he smiled easily, rather than barely managing to lengthen the thin line of his mouth a millimeter. Life was good. He could hardly wait to see what was going to happen next.

THE END
of an Original Gold Medal Collection by
Kurt Vonnegut, Jr.